Praise for the Bluford Series:

"As soon as I finished one book, I couldn't wait to start the next one. No books have ever made me do that before."
— *Terrance W.*

"The suspense got to be so great I could feel the blood pounding in my ears."
— *Yolanda E.*

"Once I started reading them, I just couldn't stop, not even to go to sleep."
— *Brian M.*

"These books are SO REAL. What you see in these books really happens. That's why you can't stop reading."
— *Phillip C.*

"The last thing I wanted to do was read a Bluford book or any book. But after a few pages, I couldn't put the book down. I felt like I was a witness in the story, like I was inside it."
— *Ray F.*

"I found it very easy to lose myself in these books. They kept my interest from beginning to end and were always realistic. The characters are vivid, and the endings left me in eager anticipation of the next book."
— *Keziah J.*

"I like the Bluford Series because it's action-packed all the way through."

—*Adam F.*

"My school is just like Bluford High. The characters are just like people I know. These books are real!"

—*Jessica K.*

"I thought the Bluford Series was going to be boring, but once I started, I couldn't stop reading. I had to keep going just to see what would happen next. I have to admit I enjoyed myself. Now I'm done, and I can't wait for more books."

—*Jamal C.*

"When I finished these books, I went back to the beginning and read them all over again. That's how much I loved them."

— *Caren B.*

"I've been reading these books for the last three days and can't get them out of my mind. They are that good!"

—*Stephen B.*

"I have never been so interested in any type of book in my entire life. I'm just surprised to see how much they catch my attention. Once I started reading, I could not stop. I was up all the way into the midnight hours trying to finish. The Bluford books didn't bore me or make me feel like I was wasting my time. I'm so glad I found them."

—*Desiree G.*

Summer of Secrets

Paul Langan

Series Editor: Paul Langan

TOWNSEND PRESS

Books in the Bluford Series

Copyright © 2004 by Townsend Press, Inc.
Printed in the United States of America

9 8 7 6 5 4

Townsend Press, Inc.
1038 Industrial Drive
West Berlin, New Jersey 08091

ISBN 1-59194-018-4

Library of Congress Control Number:
2003110890

Chapter 1

"I can't do this again, Carl. I don't have the strength, not without Mama."

Darcy Wills hid in the dark hallway listening to the sound of her mother's weary voice. It was 11:00 at night, and Mom was in the bedroom talking with Dad. Their door was closed. But through the thin walls of her family's small house, Darcy could hear them as if they were standing right in front of her.

"So what are you trying to say?" Dad asked. His voice was strained, as if he was carrying a heavy block of cement on his back.

Darcy stood still as a statue, careful not to make a sound that would alert her parents to the fact that she was just a few feet away in the dark.

"I don't know, Carl," Mom answered.

"I don't know anything anymore."

There was a moment of silence, and Darcy thought she heard her mother sob.

"I just don't have a good feeling about any of this."

So it *was* true, Darcy thought. Something was definitely wrong with her parents. Darcy had sensed it for days. She had noticed tension between them and had even heard Mom snap a few times, but until now she figured her mother was still recovering from the loss of Grandma.

Only three weeks ago, after a slow, steady decline in her health, Grandma had died in her sleep in the bedroom at the end of the hallway. The loss left a depressing void in the house. But in the three weeks that had passed, the sadness was replaced by an uncomfortable silence, one Darcy couldn't understand.

"Just don't worry about it, Darce," said her sister Jamee last week. Jamee was fourteen, two years younger than Darcy. "Anyway, it's none of your business. Besides, Mom's tough, and Dad's here. They'll be okay."

Darcy had rolled her eyes at her sister's comment. Jamee wasn't the best person to judge a situation. Only six months ago, she had dated Bobby Wallace, a sixteen-year-old who messed with drugs, hit Jamee, and convinced her to shoplift for him.

"How can you be so sure?" Darcy had asked.

Jamee shrugged off the question. "You know what your problem is, Darcy? You think too much," she said and then left to go to the movies with her friend Cindy Gibson. It was what Jamee always did when anything serious confronted her. Run away. Hide. Ignore it. Anything to avoid things that were unpleasant or difficult. It was Jamee's way, not Darcy's.

No, the problem is that you don't think enough, Darcy thought as she watched her sister leave. No matter what Jamee said, Darcy knew the issue with her parents was serious. For weeks, Mom had walked around in a daze, sometimes, it seemed, on the verge of tears.

Yesterday, Darcy even spotted her watching what she hated most—a TV show about a hospital emergency room. For as long as Darcy could remember, Mom had forbidden all medical shows when she was around.

"I see that stuff every day at work. I'm not going to watch it when I'm home," she had once declared. Mom was an emergency room nurse. Though she rarely discussed what she saw at the hospital, Darcy knew that her mother witnessed victims of shootings, stabbings, car accidents, and all sorts of diseases. No wonder she didn't want to see it on TV. But last night, she did not even seem to notice the TV doctors trying to revive a patient who had a heart attack. It was as if her mind was somewhere else. As if she wasn't in the room, even though her body was sprawled across the couch.

But tonight, Mom was even worse. Her face looked worn when she came home from the hospital. It wasn't the usual tiredness that made her stretch out on the couch and sleep after she got home. It was deeper, as if Mom's spirit was drained like an old battery.

"Are you all right?" Darcy had asked as Mom came in the front door, slumped onto the living room sofa, and sighed. She had not even said hello to Dad, who was making dinner for her in the kitchen.

"I'm fine," Mom grumbled. Her voice

4

had a hollow sound to it, as if she didn't believe her own words.

Darcy was certain her parents were having serious problems. That had to be why Mom was acting so strange. The last time Darcy had witnessed her parents fighting was when she was in middle school, just before her father left. There was the same tension in the house then, the same awkward silence.

"Are you sure you're okay, Mom?" Darcy had asked, hoping her mother would explain what was bothering her. Darcy couldn't help remembering the August day years ago when Dad took her and Jamee out for ice cream. She recalled the pained look on his face and the heavy drag of his steps on the concrete. It was the last thing he did with them before he took off, before the five-year span without a phone call, a birthday card, or a single word.

Mom cried every night for a month when Dad left. Seeing her so upset was almost worse than losing Dad. It was a kind of torture that made Darcy shudder whenever she remembered it. Only Grandma's strength enabled Mom to work full time, pay the bills, and hold the family together. Now Grandma was gone, and Darcy knew that if her parents split up again, there would be no one for Mom to turn to.

"Yes, I'm sure!" Mom snapped. "I'm just tired. You understand? And you know the one thing that bothers me most when I'm tired? It's people asking me what's wrong."

"Sorry," Darcy said, stepping back. She had not expected Mom to get so angry. It was just more proof that there were major problems in the family.

For the rest of the evening, Mom didn't say a word, even when Jamee came home a half hour late from the movies.

"Cindy's mom was late picking us up," Jamee explained as soon as she walked in.

Darcy did not believe her sister. There was something rehearsed about what she said, as if she had practiced it a few times. But Mom didn't even acknowledge Jamee, who quickly grabbed the cordless phone from the kitchen and retreated into her room.

For two hours, except for the TV, everything was unnaturally quiet. But Darcy knew it was a false calm, like the muffled silence just before a bad storm.

As soon as her parents headed into the bedroom, Darcy turned out the lights, locked the doors, and crept into the hallway to find out what was wrong. Now she stood outside her parents' bedroom, trying to catch pieces of their private conversation.

"What can I say to make you feel better about this?" Dad said. Darcy could feel the strain in his voice. He was upset.

"There's nothing you can say," Mom replied. "I'm too old for this, and I don't want to be in this situation. I just can't do it again, Carl. I just can't."

Suddenly Jamee's bedroom door opened, and she stepped into the hallway. Darcy turned and tried to act as if she was walking toward her own bedroom.

"What are you doing?" Jamee whispered, nearly running into Darcy.

"Just going to bed."

"No you're not. You're listening to Mom and Dad, aren't you?"

"*No*," Darcy whispered. "And keep your voice down."

"Darcy, you're the worst liar. Even in the dark, I can tell you aren't telling the truth. Why don't you just leave them alone?"

"Because something is wrong, Jamee. I know it. They didn't say a word to each other at dinner tonight, and even you had to notice that Mom's been out of it. I'm just worried."

"Maybe she's just in a bad mood or something," Jamee said, but her whisper cracked. Darcy could see Jamee's eyes dart back and forth in the darkness. She was shaking her head the way she always did when she was upset.

Though Jamee talked tough, Darcy knew that her younger sister looked up to Dad more than anyone in the world. Jamee would take it harder than anyone if Mom and Dad were having problems.

"I hope that's all it is, Jamee," Darcy said, though she was sure it wasn't. And she suspected Jamee felt the same way.

Jamee walked into the kitchen, hung up the phone she had grabbed earlier, and poured herself a glass of water. Darcy followed her.

"Why can't things just be easy for once?" Jamee said, leaning against the kitchen wall.

The two were silent for a second. Darcy wished Grandma was there to talk to. Or that Hakeem, her ex-boyfriend, was somewhere nearby so she could call him. But Grandma was gone, dead from a massive stroke, and Hakeem was living in Detroit, far away from their crowded neighborhood in southern California.

"I don't wanna think about something bad happening with Mom and Dad. I just can't deal with that," Jamee confessed between sips of water.

"Like you said. Maybe it's not that bad," Darcy replied, trying to keep her sister's spirits up.

"Yeah right," Jamee whispered bitterly. "When are things around here ever better than you expected?"

Before Darcy could reply, her sister turned and walked out of the kitchen. "I'm going to bed," Jamee said as she left. A second later, her bedroom door closed with a soft thud.

Darcy stood at the edge of the dark hallway and listened.

The house was deathly quiet, as if everything had been swept under a heavy blanket of gloom. Reluctantly, she decided to go to bed too.

Lying in bed, Darcy stared at the shadowy ceiling of her room, unable to relax. It was so quiet she could hear the rhythmic click of her watch on the other side of the room.

Tick tick tick. Like the heartbeat of some unwanted guest.

Darcy's body was tired from a full day of work at Scoops, the new ice cream parlor not far from Bluford High, where she had just finished her sophomore year. But her mind was wide awake, as if she had just drunk ten cups of coffee.

It had been this way for days, even before she noticed the strange tension between her parents. As soon as it got quiet and she was ready to go to sleep, Darcy would remember the afternoon weeks ago, when she was attacked by Brian Mason.

Often the memory was so strong, it was as if he was in the room with her, pinning her down, threatening her again, making her heart race with fear.

"What's wrong with you?" Brian's words still insulted her, bouncing inside her mind like ricocheting bullets. When he attacked, Darcy had struggled to free herself, but Brian's grip was strong, like a vise crushing her arm. Sometimes, she still felt the pain from where he had pinned her against the couch in his

apartment.

"Stop it!" she had demanded. "Let me go."

It had been a nightmare that caught Darcy completely off-guard. She had met Brian just before summer vacation began when she babysat for his sister, Liselle. At first, he seemed nice, and for a time, Darcy was flattered by his attention, especially after her old boyfriend, Hakeem Randall, broke up with her. On the day of the attack, Brian invited her to spend time alone with him, and she agreed, lying to her parents so they would let her out. But once she got there, Brian started getting physical with her. Too physical.

"You're acting like a baby," Brian had yelled when Darcy tried to stop him from lifting up her shirt.

Darcy could still feel him gripping her, his wet lips pushing against her neck, his roving hands. His musky smell. On that afternoon, he had touched her more than any other boy, even Hakeem.

No one except Mom and Dad knew of the attack. Not Jamee. Not Hakeem. Not even Tarah Carson, Darcy's best friend. It was a secret, an invisible scar Darcy

11

faced alone each night.

If Dad hadn't shown up . . .

Darcy could not bear the thought, yet she couldn't escape it either. She knew the dark corner it went to. It was the same conclusion every night.

In fifth grade, just before Dad left, Darcy had gotten into a fight at school with a seventh grade boy who pulled her bra strap, making it snap painfully against her back. To the kid, it was just a joke. But Dad had seen what happened, grabbed the boy and dragged him to the principal's office.

"What's wrong with you, boy? You treat girls with respect, you hear me!" Dad had yelled, holding the kid's shirt in his clenched fist. Even the principal looked scared.

It was then Darcy knew her father would always keep her safe. Would protect her when she needed it. Would never allow anyone to hurt her. Dad had proved that again when Brian attacked. He had saved her. He had stopped Brian from going any further. He had found her and brought her home.

But now, with her parents fighting, it seemed Dad might not always be there. Maybe he would go away again, perhaps

12

for good.

Darcy trembled in her bed.

If Dad hadn't shown up . . .

If Dad wasn't there . . .

If Dad leaves again . . .

Darcy's mind raced, as it had each night for the past week. In the shadows, she could almost feel the specter of Brian watching her. And even though she knew he was gone, that he had moved over 300 miles away to Oakland to live with his aunt, Darcy still could not shake the damage he had done, the crack he had put in her world, one that left voices deep inside her which she could not silence.

"You're not safe," the voices said. *"Boys can't be trusted. The world is dangerous. Your father won't always be there to protect you."*

Chapter 2

"Can I help you?" Darcy asked the customer standing at the counter. She did her best to sound cheerful, but it wasn't easy. She was tired from not sleeping, and her mind was on her parents, not her job at Scoops.

Darcy had been working there for more than a week already. Dad had suggested she apply for the job when he saw a "Help Wanted" sign in the window. Located next door to Niko's Pizza, her favorite hangout, Scoops seemed as good a place as any to work.

The same day Dad mentioned Scoops, Liselle Mason had called to ask Darcy to come back to work babysitting. She assured Darcy that Brian was far away in Oakland and that he would be there all summer. Still, Darcy refused the offer, breaking into a cold sweat at the sound of Liselle's voice. There was no way she would go back to Liselle's apartment. Not after what happened. Never.

Tamika Ardis, the manager at Scoops, called Darcy the same day she dropped off her application.

"You had the neatest application I've ever seen. If you want the job, it's yours. You can start tomorrow," Tamika had said.

After a few hours of training, Darcy was working an eight-hour shift, wearing the white visor and the bright green "Scoops" apron. The outfit was so corny, Darcy was embarrassed to put it on. But her best friend, Tarah Carson, stopped her from complaining the other night when the two talked.

"Girl, just be glad you got a job. Ain't nothin' embarrassin' about that. I'd rather get paid to wear a dumb hat than to sit around all summer without a job," Tarah had said. She worked full-time at the Brown Street Community Center. The center had a medical clinic and offered classes and job training programs for people in the neighborhood. It also had a daycare center, The Little

Learning Spot, where Tarah worked.

"Yes, I would like a medium vanilla and chocolate twist," said the middle-aged man in front of her. "Could you make it quick? I'm in a hurry."

Darcy grabbed a medium cone, went back to the large steel machine, pulled the silvery lever, and filled the cone with soft ice cream. She was careful to twist the ice cream perfectly, exactly as Tamika taught her.

"Here you go," she said, gently handing him the cone.

"Oh, that's not enough. Give me a large instead." The man looked at Darcy as if she held a rotten piece of food in her hand.

Darcy took the cone back, put it on a paper dish, and gave the man a fake smile.

"Whatever you say," she said, wishing she could dump the cone on the guy's head. Now into her second week, she was surprised to see how rude people could be.

The man took the large cone without even a thank-you. He didn't leave any money in the tip jar either.

What a jerk, she thought.

"What's wrong with everyone today?

That's the third guy I've seen today who's been rude. It's like they all decided to come in at the same time," said Haley, Darcy's coworker. Haley's blond hair was pulled into a long ponytail behind her head. She almost made the Scoops uniform look nice. Almost.

"I know what you mean, Haley. If I get one more jerk, I think I'm gonna quit."

Just then, Darcy heard the rumble of a loud car engine. Outside, a yellow Mazda sports car with fat, chrome-rimmed wheels pulled up in front of Scoops. A tall, dark-skinned young man wearing baggy jeans and a black T-shirt stepped from the car. He held a cell phone which he talked into loudly. Silvery sunglasses covered his eyes like tiny mirrors, so Darcy could not see where he was looking. As he approached the door, he moved as if he expected the world to step out of his way. Darcy turned to Haley and rolled her eyes. There was no way he was going to be nice.

"Here we go again," Haley said.

"Girl, would you come on? I ain't got all day," the guy said as he walked in. He was talking to a young woman who was right behind him. The woman was curvy, wearing denim shorts cut high to show off her long legs. Her shirt was a tight tank top that left the lower part of her stomach exposed. Darcy noticed a tiny gold hoop glittering from the girl's stomach. She had her belly button pierced.

Several customers at a front table in the ice cream store turned to get a good look. The outfit was almost small enough to be a bathing suit.

"Man, she's *fine*," mumbled a customer.

At first, Darcy didn't recognize the girl but as she came closer and took off her sunglasses, Darcy nearly fainted. She was no stranger. It was Brisana Meeks!

From middle school through their freshman year at Bluford, Brisana had been Darcy's best friend. But everything changed last year when Darcy started hanging out with Tarah, Hakeem, and Cooper. Since then, the two barely talked, and when they did, it was tense. Darcy was convinced Brisana hated her, but then weeks ago, Brisana had tried to warn her about Brian. After that, she came to Grandma's funeral. Now Darcy didn't know what to think.

"Brisana," Darcy said, trying to ignore the revealing clothes her old friend was wearing, "how are you doin'?"

"Darcy? Is that you? I didn't know you worked here," Brisana said, flashing a superior grin. "Nice uniform."

Darcy could not believe her ears. Brisana had no room to talk about clothes, not the way she was dressed. Never had she shown so much skin. Not even at the beach last summer when she was trying to attract guys.

"I just started last week. The uniforms aren't great, but you get used to it." She paused, trying to think of something else to say. If she kept talking about clothes, she knew she would slip and say something about Brisana's outfit. Something Brisana might not want to hear, especially with the guy standing right over her as if she was his property. "So . . . how's your summer going?" Darcy asked, trying to fill the awkward silence.

"It's the best summer ever, Darce. I'm working three nights a week at the Golden Grill. The tips are good, and that's where I met Duane. He's back from his first year of *college*. Can you

19

believe it? We've been to the beach twice already. He's got the best car. We even went to a club the other night. I've never had this much fun. Remember those summers when we used to sit in the house all day hoping for something to do? Not for me anymore. I'm done with that," Brisana said, glancing at the guy standing behind her.

Darcy thought something about Brisana's voice was too forced, but she wasn't sure. Brisana had always been a show-off, but never to the point where she would change her own style. Now she looked like someone out of a tacky music video.

"What about you, Darce? It can't be easy without Hakeem," Brisana said, as if she enjoyed the fact that Darcy wasn't seeing anyone.

Darcy cringed. For years, she and Brisana had competed in school. Last year, Brisana even tried to steal Hakeem away. But now that he was gone for good, Brisana's question seemed almost cruel, as if it was designed to make Darcy feel bad.

"Yo, I hate to ruin your reunion, but can we hurry it up? My pops is expecting me back at the station soon," Duane cut in, looking at Brisana.

Darcy blinked in surprise at the comment. Next to her, she noticed Haley's eyes widen. She knew exactly what Haley was thinking. *Another rude person.*

"Yeah, sure. Sorry," Darcy said, fighting the urge to tell Duane off. "What do you want?"

"We'll take two mint smoothies," he said, his bassy voice deep and flat. For a second, Darcy caught him glancing up and down at her body. It made her feel uncomfortable, especially with Brisana standing right there.

Darcy rushed to get the smoothies. When she came back, Duane had his hand on Brisana's hip, and she was leaning back into him. The two were in the middle of a slow kiss. It was as if they didn't notice they were standing in a public place with people watching them. Darcy felt embarrassed.

Last summer, Brisana talked about girls who were too forward with their boyfriends in public. "Low-class," she would call them. Now she had become just like them.

"Here you go," Darcy interrupted, trying not to stare as she handed them their order.

"Keep the change," he said, leaving an extra quarter on the counter as if he was being generous.

"*Thanks.*"

"Bye, Darcy. Call me sometime," Brisana said, heading out the door with Duane.

Several men in the store turned to watch her stroll to the car outside.

"You know her?" Haley asked, as soon as the door closed.

"Yeah," Darcy said, shocked at how much her old friend had changed. "At least, I used to."

"I'd say she's just a little over her head," Haley added, wiping the counter and putting Duane's quarter in the tip cup.

"I think you might be right."

The whole scene made Darcy's stomach twinge. Outside, the Mazda did a U-turn in front of the store and raced off in a yellow blur of speed and noise.

Too fast, Darcy thought to herself. Everything was going too fast.

"I couldn't believe it, Tarah," Darcy said to Tarah later that night, describing Brisana's behavior and what happened at Scoops. The two were at Niko's. Darcy had just gotten off work and agreed to meet Tarah and Cooper for pizza. Cooper was late, so Darcy and Tarah ordered a pizza and started eating. "There they were standing in line practically going at it."

"That's just nasty," Tarah said. "Ain't nobody wanna see that while they're trying to have their ice cream."

"I never saw the guy before, but I have to say there was something about Brisana that didn't seem right. It was like she was just doing what *he* wanted. She's normally annoying, but she's never acted that way," Darcy said, grabbing a slice of the hot pizza.

"Lotsa girls think they gotta be someone else when they go out with a boy. It's sad. You see 'em dressin' different and talkin' different, hopin' that some boy's gonna like them. It ain't right, but that's the way it is for some girls," Tarah said, taking a sip from her drink.

"I had a cousin who was smarter than anyone," she continued, "but when she hung around boys, she pretended to be dumb. I was like, 'Girl, if a boy likes you because he thinks you're dumb, then he's the wrong boy for you.' Look at

23

Coop. He knows I ain't perfect. But he likes me for me. I don't gotta be anything or anyone else. Same is true for him. Lord knows he ain't perfect, but that's all right. 'Cause he's Coop, and I don't want him any other way," Tarah said, wiping the pizza grease from her fingers.

Darcy sipped her glass of ginger ale. "So what should I do about Brisana, Tarah? Do I say something to her, or just let her alone?"

"It all depends on how serious it is," Tarah said. "I mean, me and Brisana don't mix, but if you think it's serious, you should say something to her. But I'll tell you what. I know that girl well enough to know she ain't gonna listen to you."

"Yeah. But at least I'll know that I did the right thing."

"There you go, girl. Always lookin' out for everyone else. But what about you? How's your sister doin'? I saw her the other night."

"Really?"

"Yeah, she was over Coop's house. I think she and his little brother, Desmond, are a thing."

"What?" Darcy could not believe her ears. "Are you for real?"

"Yeah, they been hangin' out a lot the past week. They're so cute. They remind me of me and Coop back in the day. Dez can't spend enough time with her. If it was up to him, they'd always be together."

Darcy felt her pulse quicken in her temples. The idea of her sister out alone with a boy, even Coop's brother, bothered her. And she did not like being the last to know what Jamee was up to. No wonder Jamee was always on the phone.

"Darcy, are you okay?"

"Yeah, I'm fine. Just thinking of something, that's all."

"It's Hakeem, isn't it? I know it's hard not having him around," she said, her eyes wide and sincere. "Just remember, Darce, you can't stop living now that Hakeem's gone. You gotta make sure you don't sit around feelin' sorry for yourself. That won't help anything."

"I know, Tarah," Darcy said, smiling weakly. It was true she missed Hakeem, but that wasn't what was bothering her now.

"Listen up. We're havin' a little cookout at the park on July 4th. My cousin Troy is coming. You two need to meet. He's school-smart like you, and he's a junior at Lincoln. I think you two might really get along."

"That's okay, Tarah," Darcy said. "I don't—"

"C'mon, girl! What have you got to lose?"

"But Tarah—"

"Darcy, it'll be fun. Coop's gonna be there. We'll have burgers and hot dogs. I'm gonna make my famous chicken. There's gonna be fireworks. You gotsta be there with us. Besides, it'll do you some good to get outside."

The last thing Darcy wanted was Tarah to fix her up with someone. After Brian, she wasn't ready to deal with any boy, not even Tarah's cousin. She knew what the night would be like. Tarah and Cooper would be watching her every move, waiting for some spark with Troy. They would be on display, like the dead frogs in her biology class, pinned up in front of everyone so they could be examined, studied, analyzed. Darcy wanted no part of that.

Darcy knew Tarah had no clue why the idea of meeting a boy bothered her. Tarah didn't know about Brian, or her nightly terrors, her inability to sleep. And sitting in Niko's, Darcy was not about to tell her now. Perhaps not ever. The memories were bad enough. But the idea of others, her friends, knowing how vulnerable she had been was ten times worse. It filled her with shame, making her blush.

"Well? Spit it out, girl. Why you look like you just ate a piece of bad pizza?"

Darcy cringed and tried to think of a lie to tell her best friend.

Chapter 3

Just then, Tarah looked up over Darcy's shoulder. "It's about time," she said suddenly. "Where you been at, Coop?"

Darcy was grateful to see Cooper Hodden, Tarah's boyfriend. She hoped Tarah would drop the subject of the cookout.

As Cooper approached the table, Darcy noticed he smelled of grease. A hand-shaped smudge of oil was streaked across the bottom of his dark blue work shirt. What surprised Darcy most was the angry scowl on his face. She had never seen him look so mad. Normally he was one of the friendliest people Darcy knew. Yet now he almost looked scary.

"Wassup, ladies," he grumbled,

grabbing a chair. "Man, I had the *worst* day."

"What happened?" Tarah asked.

"It's Duane Nye. If I have to work with him all summer, I think I'ma go crazy. I don't care if he's in college. Me and that punk are gonna have problems."

"Calm down, Coop. Tell us what happened," Tarah insisted. "Right now you're soundin' like a thug or something."

Cooper leaned back and rubbed his forehead as if he had a headache. For the past two summers, he had been working as an assistant at Nye's Garage, an auto repair shop not far from his house. Darcy knew he planned to become a mechanic. He had joked about it many times.

"The way I see it, people always gonna need someone to fix their cars. So, if I become a mechanic, I'll always have work and get paid. One day, there's gonna be a Coop's Car Center in every neighborhood. People in like Kansas or Alaska or something will see my mug on a poster and say, 'We gotsta go to Coop's to get our car fixed,'" Cooper kidded once, but Darcy believed him.

Cooper might not have been the best student at Bluford, but he had more street smarts than anyone Darcy knew. He also had the magic ability to get along with almost everyone. And Cooper was already a skilled mechanic. He kept his old pickup truck running like brand new. Darcy had gone many places in the truck, thanks to Cooper's skill. Yet now, sitting at the table, he seemed ready to break something, not fix it.

"The problem ain't my job. It's Duane, the owner's son. Since that boy got back from college, he acts like he can run the place, looking down at the rest of us like he's better than we are. Just 'cause he went to prep school and his dad's got money," Cooper said, shrugging his shoulders.

"What happened, Coop?"

"Dude lied and got me in trouble. That's what happened."

"Huh?"

"This afternoon, Mr. Nye asked me to set up three giant displays full of oil cans. It took me two hours to get it exactly the way he wanted them. Then Duane comes along, knocks the display over, and blames it on me. Cans were rolling everywhere, knocking into things. It was embarrassing, and Mr. Nye thinks it's my fault."

"Why don't you tell him what Duane did?" Darcy asked.

"I tried, but he don't wanna listen to me or anyone right now. He lets Duane run the show. Dude don't do jack around the place except cause trouble and boss us around. None of the guys want to say anything 'cause they're afraid they'll lose their jobs, so they keep their mouths shut."

"I think you should just quit. That job ain't worth you being upset all summer. This is the third time Duane started trouble with you," Tarah said. "Besides, there's got to be some other place you can work, Coop."

"I know what you're sayin', but I'm not runnin' away from him. Mr. Nye ain't that bad, and Duane'll be headed back to college in the fall anyway, so I just gotta stick it out until then. But I'll tell you, if he keeps pushin' me, one of these days, I'm gonna push back."

"You stop talkin' like that, Coop," Tarah cut in. "That Duane can't get to you unless you let him. He can do and say whatever he wants, but that don't mean you gotta let it get to you."

"Girl, I am tryin', but it ain't easy," Cooper said bitterly. He went on for several minutes about Duane, and how he was always on his cell phone talking to girls while he was supposed to be working. "Dude is nothin' but a show-off. It's like everything he does is just to let everyone else know that he's the man. His yellow sports car. His expensive sunglasses. Even his girlfriends are like that."

Something in Darcy's mind clicked. Darcy had never met Duane Nye, but the description sounded familiar. Too familiar.

"Yeah, well his daddy's money and college don't make him a man. Just 'cause he didn't go to Bluford, don't mean he's any better than the rest of us. Sounds like someone needs to tell him that, you know what I'm sayin'?" Tarah said, crossing her arms on her chest.

"You got that right," Cooper nodded. "But while I'm working there, it ain't gonna be me."

"I can't believe it," Darcy said finally. "Coop, was Duane wearing a black shirt today?"

"Yeah, how'd you know?"

"Does he drive a yellow Mazda?"

"Girl, are you psychic or somethin'?"

Tarah asked.

Darcy's heart sank.

"No, I saw him today at Scoops. He's the one who's goin' out with Brisana Meeks."

"Oh, no. She didn't just say that," Cooper said, glancing briefly at Tarah. "Girl, are you serious?"

"Mmmm hmm, she's serious all right," Tarah replied, absorbing what Darcy had just said. "Darcy was just telling me that Duane and Brisana were puttin' on a show for everybody."

"A show?"

"They were all over each other in front of everyone at Scoops."

"*For real*? Aw, that's *nasty*."

"It was gross, Coop," Darcy agreed. "Real gross."

"Man, you know Tarah and I don't like Brisana, but she's datin' the wrong person. That dude is no good."

Tarah turned to Darcy and shook her head. "I guess you got the answer to your question. You have to talk to her. But I still doubt she's gonna listen."

Darcy nodded. "You're probably right, but I gotta try. She would do it for me," Darcy admitted, remembering the day Brisana tried to warn her about

Brian. Tarah and Cooper looked at each other as if they were confused by Darcy's comment.

"Are you sure?" Cooper asked finally. "I don't mean to be rude, Darcy. But the last thing I remember Brisana doing for you was when she tried to break you and Hakeem up. She don't seem to care about anyone but herself."

"Coop, why you gotta bring that old stuff up?" Tarah snapped.

"I'm just sayin' the truth. That girl don't have a nice bone in her body."

"You're wrong, Coop. You used to say the same thing about me before we became friends, and look at us now," Darcy said. Both of them turned and looked at her as if she was speaking another language. "Brisana's rude sometimes, but she's not a bad person. She came to my grandmother's funeral, and I know for a fact that if she thought I was in trouble, she'd try to help me. I gotta do the same thing for her."

"Whatever you say, girl. It's all you," Cooper replied, looking a little hurt.

Darcy felt Tarah studying her. She looked like she spotted something that disturbed her, yet she was quiet for several long seconds. Darcy looked at her watch. It was nearly 9:00.

"So you gonna be with us on July 4th or what?" Tarah asked, breaking the silence.

Darcy hesitated. She did not want to go, but she had no excuse. She could feel Tarah's and Cooper's eyes boring into her.

"Come on, Darcy. Jamee's gonna be there with Dez," Cooper added.

Darcy shifted uncomfortably in her seat. Cooper hadn't meant anything by his comment, but it annoyed her that he knew more about Jamee than she did. Worse was the idea that Tarah and Cooper had talked about hooking her up with Tarah's cousin. Like she had become some kind of charity case, someone to be pitied.

But what bothered Darcy most was what she couldn't bring herself to admit to Tarah or Cooper. The invisible grip that Brian's assault had on her life.

Darcy felt as if she was trapped in an enormous web.

"Yeah," Darcy said reluctantly, burying her deepest thoughts from her closest friends. "I'll be there."

Tarah said nothing, sipping her soda in unusual silence.

"Why didn't you tell me you were dating Desmond Hodden?" Darcy asked Jamee as soon as she got home from Scoops. She found her sister lying on her bed reading a magazine, the cordless phone next to her. Darcy knew she was waiting for a phone call.

"'Cause it's none of your business, Darcy," Jamee said, annoyance in her voice. "You're not Mom. I don't have to ask permission from you. Besides, when you started seein' that guy Brian after Hakeem moved away, I didn't see you talking to anyone about it. You still don't mention it, so don't start lecturing me about how I gotta tell you everything that I do."

Darcy winced. What Jamee said was true, but she had no idea why Darcy hadn't mentioned the details about what really happened with Brian the last time they were together.

"Just don't go there, Jamee. It's completely different."

"It's *not* different, Darce, and you know it. Ever since Grandma got sick, you started treating me like I'm just a kid who's always doing something wrong. Like I need you as a babysitter

36

24-7 or something. Sometimes I swear it's like you think you're perfect, and I'm just a total screw-up," Jamee said, tossing the magazine aside.

"That's not what I am saying," Darcy said, trying to calm her sister's growing anger. "It's just that . . . sometimes you get in over your head."

"I knew it! You always go back there. Yeah, I did some dumb stuff last year. I admit it. But that's ancient history now. It was almost a year ago when all that happened. I can't believe you're still draggin' that out every time we get into an argument."

"Try six months ago, Jamee."

"Whatever," Jamee hissed, as if just talking to Darcy was exhausting. "So what do you want, Darcy? Do I need to check in with you wherever I go? Maybe ask permission so Dez and I can go somewhere? 'Cause if that's what you want, you ain't getting it," Jamee declared defiantly.

Darcy shook her head. Part of her understood what Jamee was saying. And it was true that Desmond Hodden was someone Darcy could easily keep an eye on. But then another part of her could not get away from how young her sister looked sitting on the bed. She was just fourteen, not even in high school yet. She'd be a freshman at Bluford this fall. So would Desmond.

Just the idea of Jamee being alone with a boy made Darcy's head pound with worry. She could almost see someone like Brian trying to get Jamee alone. It was as if her nightmare had been recorded on a tape that played over and over in Darcy's head.

"Jamee, all I want is for you to be careful with whatever it is you're doing, okay?"

"I'm not stupid, Darcy. I know about guys. I'm not going to run off somewhere with someone I don't know."

Darcy stepped back and glared at her sister. Jamee's words hit her like a kick in the stomach. "Who are you to start calling other girls stupid? You're only fourteen years old! Women who know a lot more than you get in trouble each day because of guys, so don't start acting like you're Miss Know-It-All."

Jamee's jaw dropped. She looked stunned by Darcy's outburst. "What's your problem tonight? You're acting crazy. We're talking about Dez Hodden, not some stranger."

Darcy took a deep breath and tried to diffuse the anger that surged in her chest. "You don't know everything that can happen, Jamee. So be smart. Tell someone what you're up to just in case something happens, and don't judge other girls who get caught up in boy troubles. They may be closer to you than you think," she said.

"Darcy, are you all right? Your eyes . . . are you crying?"

"*No,*" she said firmly, rubbing her eyes, feeling the moisture in her hands. "I'm just tired, that's all. I need to go to bed." Darcy left Jamee and headed to her own bedroom, dreading the night to come. The panic and night sweats would be back.

Darcy could feel them coming on like a bad fever.

Chapter 4

"Brisana, come to the mall with me," Darcy said the next morning, trying to forget her exhaustion and the nearly sleepless night which had finally ended. It was late morning, and she was pacing back and forth across her bedroom, the cordless phone pressed up against the side of her face. "It'll be like old times. I even have enough money to buy something."

"*Today*?" Brisana asked. "Duane is supposed to pick me up at 6:00. We're going to the movies."

"We can go early. We can get some lunch at the food court, and you'll be back in time."

"How are we going to get there?"

"Like old times. The bus," Darcy replied.

"*The bus*?" Brisana repeated as if the words were somehow offensive. "I never take the bus anymore."

"It's what we always did. Come on. It'll be fun."

"The *bus*?" Brisana scoffed. "*Fun*?"

"Brisana, would you stop being a snob and just come with me!" Darcy snapped.

The phone was silent for several long seconds, and Darcy wondered whether the serious conversation with Brisana would have to happen over the phone.

"All right, relax," Brisana replied finally. "I'll meet you at the bus stop in an hour."

Darcy got to the bus stop early and watched as Brisana crossed the street to meet her. She was happy to see that her old friend was wearing jeans and a loose-fitting T-shirt, nothing like the outfit she had worn the day before.

"I knew you'd be early," Brisana said, sitting down on the wooden bench and looking at her reflection in a tiny mirror she carried in her purse. "Some things never change."

"You too, girl. How many times have I seen you staring at that mirror?" Darcy teased. She couldn't remember the last time the two went out, but she was sure that when they did, Brisana had stopped at some point to examine her makeup.

"What can I say? I just wanna look good, especially now that I'm seeing Duane," Brisana admitted, putting the tiny mirror away.

"You always look good, Brisana. I don't think I've ever seen you look bad."

"You just aren't looking close enough," Brisana said matter-of-factly. "Duane says my face is getting heavier, and I think he's right. What do you think? Does my face look fatter to you."

"No! You look fine, Brisana. And even if it did, who is he to be complaining about it? He's only been seeing you for a week." She wanted to make Brisana question Duane, but she knew that she couldn't be too strong. Brisana wouldn't listen if she was.

"*A week?* We've been dating for a month now. Where have you been?" Brisana challenged.

Darcy was surprised that they had been going together that long, but it made sense. So much had happened to her in the last month of school that she had no idea what Brisana was up to.

"Sorry," she said. "I guess I've been a little distracted."

Brisana looked at her and smiled. "It's okay. I knew you had a lot going on at home with your grandma and all. How's your mom doing?"

"She's okay, just really tired," Darcy said, not wanting to admit her concerns about her parents to Brisana. "I think she's still getting used to Grandma not being around."

"My mom was a mess when my grandma died," Brisana said, watching a woman walk up the street. "I was so little, I can hardly remember my grandma, but I remember my mom crying in church like she was a baby. It was scary."

In the distance, Darcy could hear the growing roar of the bus coming down the busy street toward them.

"That's the worst, seeing your parents upset. I hate that," Darcy said, thinking of her mother's behavior over the past few nights.

"I guess, but I don't have to worry about that. My parents don't talk enough to get upset about anything, especially me. As long as my grades are good, and I don't come in too late, they leave me alone." Brisana spoke strangely, as if she was boasting and complaining at the same time.

The grumble of the bus grew louder and was followed by the skull-splitting whine of brakes and a cloud of sooty diesel smoke. A second later, the bus door opened with a noisy metallic clap.

"Just like old times," Darcy said with a smile, getting in line.

"You called *this* fun?" Brisana replied, her face almost in a childish pout as she boarded the bus.

The bus rolled slowly through the neighborhood, merged with the highway, and sped to the mall just outside the city. After a short walk, the two were standing right outside the food court at a giant T-shaped intersection in the heart of the mall.

Crowds of people passed them on either side, while others eyed them from the second and third floor balconies. Teenagers were everywhere. Kids from the suburbs, the city, and every place in between, all moving along slowly, some working at stores, others shopping. All of them people-watching.

"Yo, ladies, you wanna sit here with us? I'll buy you lunch," said a young light-skinned guy with dreadlocks sitting at a round table with his friends.

Darcy turned away uncomfortably. Brisana rolled her eyes but said nothing.

"Aww, c'mon. Why you gotta to be that way?" the guy added. Two other teenaged guys at the table laughed. "Just give me your digits, baby."

"You better give up, bro. You're embarrassing yourself," said one of the guys to his friend.

"Let's go," Darcy urged, suddenly feeling nervous.

"Don't worry about it, Darcy. It's no big deal," Brisana said, following her away from the food court.

Darcy nodded, saying nothing about the sudden wave of dizziness that swept over her, the nervous tremors in her hands, or the loud pounding in her chest. She had been coming to the mall with Brisana since middle school. Guys were always yelling stuff to them, especially in summer when everyone was out of school. Once or twice, they had even stopped and talked to them. Brisana would flirt, sometimes giving away a fake phone number, joking afterwards that she would never call anyone she met at the mall. It was all harmless back then, but now it made Darcy feel threatened, unsafe.

"You all right? You look like something freaked you out."

"Yeah, I'm fine. I just didn't feel like dealing with them right now," Darcy said, trying to calm herself and stop Brisana from staring at her. "I don't understand what guys are thinking when they act that way. Like I'm going to hook up with him because he yelled at me in the middle of the mall. *Please.*"

"What are you getting so upset for? Guys do that all the time."

"Yeah? Well, maybe they shouldn't," Darcy snapped, looking over her shoulder just to make sure they were alone.

"Geez, someone's having a bad day," Brisana said, putting her hand on her hip and raising one eyebrow at Darcy. "Well, I came here to do some shopping, and that's what I'm gonna do. You coming?"

Brisana strolled across the mall, and Darcy watched her, shocked at how upset she was feeling. For a second, she had wanted to run away, even though she figured the guy meant no harm. Whatever he had intended, Brisana was right. It had freaked her out. Darcy knew it had to do with the nightmares. With Brian.

Darcy followed Brisana and wondered how she would ever talk to her about Duane. Maybe she'd just do it another time, she thought. Or maybe Brisana didn't really need to talk. After all, she wasn't the one getting panicky in a mall just because of a dumb guy, Darcy thought. But then she noticed where Brisana was going.

Up on the second floor of the mall, behind Steppin', where Darcy and Tarah always bought shoes, was a shop they had often joked about, For Ladies Only. It was a store that specialized in women's clothing, especially bathing suits and sleepwear, and Darcy had passed it dozens of times but rarely went in. The place just wasn't her style. Everything seemed too frilly and cost too much.

"Coop always says he's gonna buy me something nice from there, but I tell him, 'Boy, save your money,'" Tarah once said. Hakeem never even mentioned it.

By the time Darcy got to the top of the escalator, Brisana was already heading straight through the entranceway.

What are you doing, Brisana? Darcy

thought as she stopped outside the door. Inside the front glass displays were mannequins wearing lacy nightgowns and fancy pajamas. Darcy felt a little uncomfortable looking at them. She wondered if other people were watching her.

"Ooh, look. A sale!" Brisana said excitedly, moving deeper into the store.

Reluctantly, Darcy entered. As soon as she stepped inside, she inhaled the over-powering fragrance of perfume. It was so strong, it nearly made her eyes water. A sign over the cash register showed a picture of a tiny bottle next to a woman's stomach.

"Heat. The new scent of summer. On sale now for $29.99."

No thanks, Darcy thought to herself. The scent reminded her of a mixture of overripe strawberries and smoke.

The walls to her left and right were painted blood red and lined with lacy curtains in pink and beige, making the whole place look like a strange fake mansion. On the back wall hung a series of black and white posters of skinny women with long legs. Darcy had been to the store a few times. Her Aunt Charlotte had even bought her a pair of expensive pajamas from the store for Darcy's fifteenth birthday.

"This is real silk," Aunt Charlotte had said. "Now that you're a young woman, you should have something nice. This is what a queen wears when she goes to sleep," Aunt Charlotte said when she gave her the pajamas. Darcy had worn them once and left them in the back of her drawer. Sweat pants and a cotton T-shirt were more comfortable. Up until last year, Brisana had been the same way about clothes. Yet now she moved through racks as if she had been there many times.

"Come here. Check this out," Brisana exclaimed. She was holding a white bikini that Darcy wouldn't dream of putting on. "Isn't it nice? Duane says he wants me to get a nice bathing suit. You think he'd like this?"

Darcy looked at the bathing suit again. It looked no bigger than a pair of socks. "You'd wear that for *him*?"

"Yeah," Brisana said. "Why, you think there's something wrong with it? Maybe a different color?"

Darcy shifted uncomfortably. This was her chance, though she could hear Tarah's voice in her mind. *She ain't gonna listen to you.*

"No, it's not about the bathing suit, Brisana. It's just . . ." Darcy stammered.

"Just what? Go ahead, say it."

"Don't you think you're moving just a little too fast? I mean, you hardly know Duane, and now you're wearing skimpy stuff for him."

"It's just a bathing suit!" Brisana said, her voice suddenly loud.

"But yesterday at Scoops, you two were all over each other. I've never seen you like that before. You seem so . . . different."

"Maybe 'cause now I'm happy. Did you ever think of that, *Darcy*?" Brisana said, saying her name as if it were an insult. "What do you care if I act a little different?"

"I'm your friend, Brisana. That's what friends do. They look out for each other when they see something wrong."

"Yeah, well, nothing's wrong," Brisana insisted. "The only problem is that you can't handle that I'm happy with Duane. I can understand if you're jealous. I mean I know it must be hard without Hakeem around and all, but that doesn't mean you have to get up in my face like *I* am doing something wrong."

"*Jealous*?!" Darcy exclaimed. She couldn't believe her ears.

"Think about it, Darce. Your boyfriend's gone. I've got Duane, and as sorry as it seems, even Tarah's got a boyfriend. The only one who doesn't is you, and you can't stand it."

"Girl, you are *so* wrong," Darcy said, trying to keep her cool. "What I'm tryin' to say is that Duane doesn't seem right."

"Don't even start with me, Darcy," Brisana said, shaking her head as if what she heard disgusted her. "I can't even believe you're talking to me like this. For once, I have someone that makes me feel good, and all you wanna do is mess it up. I don't even want to talk about this."

"Brisana, I'm not trying to mess anything up. I just don't want you to rush things. You know, just slow down," Darcy said.

Brisana sighed and looked at the bathing suit thoughtfully. "You know what Duane said to me? He told me he loved me. We were at the beach in his car, and he looked at me with his dark eyes and said it. I didn't know what to say."

Looking at her, Darcy knew Brisana

meant every word she said. But, at the same time, Darcy doubted that Duane's words were sincere.

"He's movin' kinda fast. Don't you think?"

"Look, Darcy, I know he's not perfect. But he says he loves me, and he takes me out. We have a good time together. What's wrong with that?"

"What do you mean he's not perfect?" Darcy said, remembering how Cindy, Jamee's friend, once said similar words about a boy who nearly beat her up one night.

"See. There you go again," Brisana said rolling her eyes. "Let's just drop it, okay."

"Are you going to purchase that?" interrupted the saleswoman from behind the cash register. The voice startled Darcy, but Brisana didn't even flinch.

"Yeah, I'll take it," she said, handing over the bikini. "That's just what I need."

The woman smiled and rang up the bathing suit as Darcy turned away, unsure of what to do next. Tarah was right. Brisana was not going to listen.

Chapter 5

On the way out of the mall, Darcy passed the food court where the guy had yelled out to her. He was gone, but her palms still got cold and clammy, and she felt a tremor when she walked by where he had been sitting.

"He's gone, Darcy. Relax. I know who you're looking for," Brisana said.

"I'm not looking for anyone," Darcy lied. She was still alarmed at how nervous she felt. Never had a trip to the mall bothered her so much.

"Mmm hmm," Brisana said, peering into her shopping bag as they walked to the bus stop. "I really hope Duane likes this."

Darcy ignored Brisana and boarded the bus, wondering what was wrong. Normally, she could talk to Grandma or to Hakeem when she had a problem, but now she had no one around to listen to her.

There was always Tarah, but Darcy didn't even know what to say to her. Everything she could think of sounded crazy.

Yeah, I am having these bad dreams. I'm not sleeping, and some guy talking to me at the mall almost made me flip out. What kind of problem was that, Darcy thought. It almost sounded silly. She knew other people who dealt with far worse problems every day. Still, she could not ignore what was happening, and Darcy knew it had everything to do with Brian. If only she could take that time back, rewind it somehow like a movie and skip it altogether. But Darcy knew that couldn't happen, that the incident had changed her.

The bus slowly returned to the neighborhood, and Darcy walked with Brisana to the end of the block where they had to split up. Brisana seemed eager to leave, checking her watch twice and picking up speed as they walked.

"I gotta go, Darcy. I want to get ready for Duane."

Darcy shrugged her shoulders. It

was almost 4:00. Brisana had plenty of time to get ready for her date with Duane, Darcy thought. She knew there was no point trying to change Brisana's mind. "Have fun," she said. "And be careful."

"Yeah okay," Brisana replied automatically. Darcy could tell by her tone that she was not listening. Her mind was already looking ahead.

"Call me. Maybe we can go out again or something."

"Bye," Brisana replied, moving quickly down the street.

Darcy turned and started walking home, wondering if maybe she should talk to her parents about what happened to her at the mall.

"How are we gonna afford things if you're not working?" Mom yelled as Darcy walked in the front door. She was talking to Dad, who sat on the living room couch massaging his temples.

"I wasn't fired. They just cut my hours, that's all," he explained.

"Yeah, well, that's not good enough, Carl, and you know it," Mom said. Her forehead, creased from worry, looked like the old wrinkled curtains in

Grandma's room. She clutched a tissue in her hand, which she occasionally brought to her eyes.

"What happened?" Darcy asked.

"Nothing, baby. Don't worry about it," Dad said, scratching his chin, staring down at the floor as if his eyes were seeing more than the faded gray carpet.

The room was suddenly quiet, and Darcy turned to her mother, who was wiping her eyes. "Will someone tell me what happened?"

Darcy's mother took a deep breath. "Business at the store where your father works is slow. The company's reducing everyone's hours. Now he's going to be working part-time instead of full-time," Mom explained, as if she was reporting a crime to Darcy.

"That's not so bad, right?" Darcy asked, remembering how the whole family used to live on Mom's income alone. "I mean we were okay for a long time when Dad wasn't around, so we should be okay now," Darcy said.

Mom turned away as if what Darcy said bothered her. On the other side of the room, Dad slowly rubbed his forehead, his face in an expression of pain. Darcy knew it hurt him to hear how much the family struggled when he left.

"I'll just get another job. It wouldn't be the first time I had two jobs."

"You know it's not that easy, Carl. Lots of people are out of work right now, and you're not a twenty-five-year-old man anymore."

"I'll find something. Even if I have to wash dishes, I'll do it," Dad insisted.

"If we have to, maybe we should go back to the apartment or something. It wasn't that bad. Jamie and I can work too," Darcy suggested. She meant every word. When Dad left years ago, Mom moved the entire family into a rundown apartment building to save money. Almost immediately, Grandma moved in and helped with everything until her first stroke. Then Darcy and Jamee took care of her while Mom worked.

They had lived in the apartment until Dad returned and convinced them to move into a small house several blocks away. Darcy remembered the day he and Mom announced that they were going to try to give their broken marriage a second chance. It was like a storybook fantasy when Dad showed them the new house. Mom had cried and almost refused to believe it was real. But then, days later, they moved in, and everything seemed perfect until Grandma's health declined. She passed away in the bedroom next to Darcy's room. Now, it seemed the rest of the fantasy was coming apart.

"No, you're not going back to the apartment," Dad grumbled.

"How do you know, Carl? At least Darcy is being realistic. That's more than I hear from you," Mom said, her voice charged with resentment.

Dad stood up abruptly and walked toward the door. "I need to take a walk," he said.

"That's not gonna help anything," Mom snapped.

"Mom, it's not Dad's fault that business is slow," Darcy said.

Her mother ignored her comment and watched as Dad opened the door.

"I'll be back," he said and walked out.

"You better be," Mom mumbled, quietly blowing her nose. A single tear snaked down her face.

Darcy knew Mom was thinking about the time Dad left for good. So was Darcy. She could not believe what was happening. It was as if her entire world was unraveling, and she was powerless to

58

stop it. Across from her, Mom sighed, closed her eyes, and leaned back in her chair.

Suddenly, the front door opened and Jamee rushed into the living room. "Hey, where's Dad going? I saw him outside walking down the street like he was in a daze or something. He didn't even hear me calling him."

Darcy watched as her mother got up without a word and trudged down the hallway into her bedroom.

"He went for a walk, Jamee," Darcy said.

"A *walk*?" Jamee asked, watching her mother close the bedroom door. "What's wrong? Why is everyone acting so strange?"

Darcy wanted to get up and go to her room too. She didn't feel like discussing everything with her sister, but Jamee looked worried. She deserved an explanation.

"Mom's upset 'cause Dad sort of got laid off. He's going to be working only part-time from now on."

Jamee was quiet for a second. Darcy knew she was thinking about what she said.

"Why's she so upset about *that*?"

Jamee asked finally, as if what Darcy described made no sense. "I mean, we were okay when Dad wasn't even here. So even if he only works part-time, that's still better than how things were before."

Darcy knew Jamee was right. Mom seemed too upset. Like the real reason for her tears was not about Dad's job, but something else. Something bigger.

"That's what I said, but she didn't want to hear that," Darcy admitted, remembering what she had heard when she listened to her parents talking in the bedroom. "I'm telling you, it's like I said last night. Something's wrong, and I know it doesn't have anything to do with Dad's work 'cause Mom was upset before she even heard the news."

"Whatever," Jamee sighed. Without another word, she sat on the couch, grabbed the remote control, and clicked on the TV. For several minutes, the two were quiet, and Jamee flipped the stations rapidly, not stopping long enough to even see what was on. It was the way Jamee dealt with problems. Don't stop. Don't think. Just keep moving so you don't get hurt or feel pain.

Though her sister always tried to

hide it, Darcy could see that Jamee was upset. It was on her face and in her eyes. Finally, she turned the TV on to *Diva Challenge*, a program where teenaged girls compete in a talent show. Darcy watched as a heavy-set girl sang an old love song.

And I will always love you, the singer sang over and over again.

The girl's voice was thin and tinny, and the song annoyed Darcy. It seemed to mock her mood. But to Darcy's surprise, it didn't bother Jamee, who turned the volume up slightly. They watched the performance without speaking.

"Do you think this song's real?" Jamee asked suddenly, the tone of her voice making her seem much younger than her fourteen years.

"What kinda question is that?" Darcy asked, unsure what her sister was getting at.

"I know it sounds corny, but do you think you always love a person? Like if a boy tells you he loves you, do you think he always will, or is it something he's just saying?"

Darcy's mind spun. It was that word again. *Love.* The same word that Brisana mentioned when she talked about Duane. Now her sister was saying it too. Darcy hated to think that Jamee was referring to her relationship with Desmond.

"I think it can be forever, but most of the time, it isn't. Put it this way, if someone I've known for only a few weeks starts telling me he loves me, I'm not buyin' it," Darcy said, hoping her answer would help Jamee.

"But what about you and Hakeem? Did you two, you know, love each other?"

Darcy suddenly felt uncomfortable. She and Hakeem were different. They had been through so much together during the previous year. And even though they broke up, Darcy hadn't fully let Hakeem go, though she never admitted it to anyone. Looking at her sister, Darcy feared an honest answer to Jamee's question might confuse her. Yes, there was love in her relationship with Hakeem, but that didn't mean it was there with Desmond. Darcy wrestled for the right words. On TV, the singer repeated the chorus even louder than before.

And I will always love you,
Will always love you . . .

"Jamee, what's wrong with you? Why are you asking me questions like this?" she responded finally, hoping to find out what her sister really wanted to know.

Jamee clicked the TV off, sat up, and turned to Darcy, her eyes bright and intense, like two flashlights.

"Because I don't know what to believe, Darcy," Jamee said. "When Dez looks at me and says he loves me, that I'm his only girl, I want to believe him. When Dad tells me he loves me and he's never gonna leave, I want to believe him too. But right now . . ." she paused, her eyes beginning to glisten. "I just don't know what to believe."

"Jamee, what Dad says and what Dez says are completely different," Darcy said, but Jamee wasn't listening. Without waiting for a reply, she jumped up, grabbed the cordless phone, and stormed into her room. Darcy leaned back in the living room chair where her grandmother used to sit. The chair was covered in a blanket Grandma had made years ago. Darcy wished she could talk to her again.

"Don't worry, Angelcake. It's all gonna be all right. You'll see," Grandma used to say, and somehow Darcy would feel better.

But Grandma was gone, and Darcy was in the living room alone.

Suddenly, the front door opened, and Dad walked back in. Darcy turned, curious to see if there was anything different about him. Part of her almost expected him to announce some horrible news.

"I'm leaving for good this time, Darcy. Take care of your Mom and sister," she could hear his voice in her head as he stepped into the living room. He seemed to notice her watching him.

"What is it? Why are you staring at me like that?"

Darcy studied his face to see if she could find any evidence to support her fears. He looked tired, but sincere. She could see he had a lot on his mind, but he seemed genuinely concerned about her. Part of her wanted to tell him about her recent nightmares, the episode at the mall, her sleepless nights and panicky feelings. But she could not bring herself to say the words, especially not with everything else happening. Still, she had to say something about the uncomfortable tension which seemed to hang over in the house like some sort of curse.

"Dad, can we talk?" she said.

Dad nodded somberly and sat down on the couch across from Darcy. He took a deep breath, as if he expected bad news from her. "What's on your mind?"

"You and Mom . . . are you guys okay?"

Her father rubbed his temples. "Yeah, we're okay, Darcy."

"Then why are the two of you always upset, and how come Mom's been crying so much?"

"Did you talk to her about it?"

"I tried, but all she says is that she's tired. I know she's not telling me every-thing. I'm not stupid," Darcy said. "Are you guys having problems again?"

"Darcy, look, you're just going to have to trust me on this. Your mother and I are dealing with a lot of stuff right now. But it's not your fault, and there is nothing you can do about it. As soon as we're ready, we'll all sit down and talk with you and Jamee about it. But right now isn't the time."

"But Dad—"

"Darcy, trust me. Right now this is

between me and your mother. When it concerns you, we'll tell you about it."

Without another word, Dad got up and headed down the hallway. A second later, Darcy heard the soft wooden thud of the bedroom door closing.

Unable to relax, Darcy walked into Grandma's room and sat on the bed where her grandmother spent her last days. The room still smelled of lilac perfume, Grandma's favorite scent. Mom had even left Grandma's shawl on the rocking chair exactly where she used to keep it. Though it had been weeks, the room felt as if Grandma had been in it just minutes ago. Darcy could almost see the rocking chair moving, hear it creak under the weight of her grandmother.

"Don't let any clouds steal your sunshine, Angelcake."

Darcy stretched on the bed and stared up at the ceiling. Even though she was in the same house with the rest of her family, Darcy felt completely alone. It was as if something was driving them apart, making them put walls between themselves, preventing them from talking. Something secret.

"Please make it okay, Grandma," Darcy prayed from Grandma's bed.

As much as she tried to stay strong, Darcy could not shake the feeling that her family was sinking toward something bad, an unstoppable slide that could drive them apart forever.

Suddenly Darcy heard the sound of footsteps rushing down the hallway. She sat up in the bed nervously.

"Darcy?" Jamee called, her voice urgent. "Where are you?"

"I'm in Grandma's room," Darcy said, getting up from the bed, unsettled by the way Jamee was calling her. "What's wrong?"

Jamee walked in and eyed Darcy strangely. "Nothing's wrong. You got a phone call, that's all. It's someone special."

"Who is it?" Darcy asked, taking the phone from her sister.

"You'll see," Jamee said, leaving her.

"Hello?"

"Hey, girl, how are you? I miss you so much," said a familiar voice.

Darcy felt as if her knees were about to give out. She put her hand against the nearest wall to steady herself.

It can't be true, she thought. But her ears told her otherwise.

Chapter 6

It was Hakeem Randall.

"Hakeem! Oh my goodness! I can't believe it's you," Darcy said. Her heart skipped a beat. She hadn't spoken to him since her grandmother's funeral, when he made a surprise trip from Detroit to be by her side.

"How is everyone back there? How are your parents?"

"They're okay," Darcy said, trying to sound upbeat. She wasn't going to go into her family's problems now, not with Hakeem paying for a long distance call. "How about your family? How's your dad?"

"Darcy, that's why I'm calling. I can't stay on the phone long, but I just wanted to give you the good news." His voice was fast and upbeat, like he could barely restrain what he had to say.

"Tell me!" she urged.

"My Dad's cancer has stopped. He's passed his physical, and he's getting a little stronger every day," Hakeem said. She could hear the excitement in his voice. It was a huge change from how he had been just months ago when he told her his father was sick and that his family was moving out to Detroit.

"That's the best news I've heard all summer!" Darcy said, meaning every word. For a second, she almost forgot about the gloomy cloud in her own house.

"There's more, Darcy. Dad plans to stay here and help my uncle, but he said this fall I could come back to Bluford."

"What? How?" Darcy almost couldn't believe the news.

"Coop's mom said I could stay with him this school year. My parents thought about it for a while, and since they've known each other for years, they said it was okay."

Darcy felt her eyes begin to tear. "Are you serious? Are you really coming back?"

"Not until the first week of September, so it'll be a while, but I wanted to tell you myself. I can't wait to see you. I miss you big time."

"I miss you too, Hakeem," Darcy said, wanting to reach out to him. She wished he was next to her so they could talk. Yet as she thought about it, she did not know what she would say. How could she ever tell him about the time she spent with Brian Mason? Would he be disappointed or blame her for what happened? Would he somehow see her differently? Think less of her because she had allowed Brian, for a time, to touch her? It was a secret she would have to keep. There was no way she would let it ruin the news of Hakeem's return.

"Well, I should go, Darcy. I just wanted to let you know. Maybe we can go to the Junior Prom next year after all," he said.

"You better ask me first," she teased.

"I think I just did."

"Then you have a date," she answered, almost laughing.

"I'm there already," he replied. She could hear other people talking to Hakeem in the background over the phone. Though there were several voices, one was clear.

"C'mon, we got work to do, cuz! You gotta hang up that phone."

Darcy listened as Hakeem yelled something and then spoke to her quickly. "I wish I had more time, Darce, but I gotta go now. I'll be there this fall. I promise," he added.

When she hung up the phone, Darcy wiped tears from her eyes. Her first boyfriend was coming back. It was the best news she had all summer, and for a time, she allowed herself to enjoy it. Like a favorite dessert eaten slowly.

The next morning, Darcy woke up totally confused. She heard the sound of women's voices coming from the living room, and she looked at the clock. It was 8:45, and Darcy didn't have to be at Scoops until noon. Since the school year ended, Darcy had started sleeping late, especially since the nightmares had begun. She wanted to roll over and go back to sleep, but the sound of the voices made it impossible. Who was talking, she wondered, getting up and heading to the edge of the door.

"I can't believe you let yourself get into this position again, Mattie. At your age?" Darcy recognized the voice immediately.

71

It was her Aunt Charlotte, Mom's sister. Charlotte had never liked Dad, and she always acted as if she was somehow better than everyone else. She lived alone in a nice townhouse outside the city, and Darcy couldn't stand her because she was always judging everything. And in her eyes, Dad, the new house, and even Jamee and Darcy's behavior never measured up.

"Look, I didn't ask you to come here today, and if all you're gonna do is tell me about my mistakes, you can just leave," Mom said.

"Now you don't have to get upset. I came here so I could go with you today, and that's what I'm going to do," Aunt Charlotte said. "Just because Carl made another mistake and can't be here doesn't mean I shouldn't be."

"Charlotte, *please*!" Mom yelled. "If I knew you were gonna be like this, I wouldn't have even called you. Now let's go. I don't want to be late."

Darcy listened as the two women walked out and locked the door behind them. The house was quiet. Jamee's door was still closed, and Dad was out already. Darcy felt a nervous tremble in her stomach. Something strange was going on.

But what?

At Scoops, business was busier than ever. For the first time in a week, the summer heat was scorching the city, making people rush in to get something cool to eat and escape the hot sun. It was so busy that Tamika, Darcy's manager, was forced to work side by side with her and Haley, just to keep the lines down.

At 4:00, Darcy noticed a yellow sports car pass by outside. It looked exactly like the one Duane drove. Minutes later, a pretty, light-skinned girl with green eyes came in wearing a UCLA T-shirt.

"Can I get two mint smoothies?" she asked.

It can't be! Darcy thought to herself. It was the same order she prepared for Brisana and Duane the other day. Darcy handed her the smoothies and collected the money, carefully studying the girl's face.

"Thank you," the girl said, walking out.

Alarm bells were going off in Darcy's head. She had to find out one way or the other if the girl had anything to do with Duane. Quickly, she turned to Haley. "I need to take a five-minute break. I'll be right back."

"*Now?*" Haley protested. "It's too busy, Darce."

"Two minutes. That's all I need," she said, taking off her apron and visor, and rushing out the door.

Outside, the hot afternoon wind blasted Darcy like exhaust from a giant furnace. The girl had already vanished. Darcy scanned up and down the main street looking for the T-shirt. While there were people everywhere, the girl was not one of them. Darcy rushed to the nearest corner. Beneath her feet, the sidewalk was hot, making the bottoms of her shoes soft and gummy.

Up ahead, about thirty yards away, she spotted the yellow sports car. The door was open, and the girl was just easing into the passenger seat. In a second, the door closed, and Darcy saw her lean toward the driver for a instant, as if she was kissing him. But the bright glare of the sun made it impossible to tell for sure. Darcy was about to move in for a closer look when the car sped off.

There was no doubt in Darcy's mind.

Duane was behind the wheel. And though she really couldn't see, Darcy was sure the girl was more than just Duane's friend.

"He's cheating on you, Brisana," Darcy said to herself, making her way back to Scoops, the anger in her chest burning like the summer sun that blazed overhead.

"Just stop it!" Brisana yelled over the phone. It was a little after 9:00 p.m., and Darcy decided she had to tell Brisana what she had seen. "I don't want to hear it."

"Brisana it's true. I saw him with my own eyes," Darcy insisted.

"Darcy this is the lowest I've ever seen you go. I know you're lonely and jealous, but I never imagined you'd do something like this."

Darcy struggled to control her temper. "Brisana, you've got to believe me. Ask Duane where he was this afternoon."

"What is your problem, Darcy?" Brisana demanded. "Even if Duane was cheating on me—which he's not—what do you care?"

Darcy paused, the words all jumbled

in her mind. "Because you would say something to me if I was seeing someone who was no good for me," Darcy said. "You did it when I saw Brian Mason, and I'm doing it for you now."

"Look, Darcy, I don't know what happened to you this summer, but you got serious issues. You were freakin' out at the mall, and now you're freakin' out at me. I don't know what your problem is, but you're just plain wrong."

Brisana's comment hit Darcy like a punch in the stomach. It was bad enough that Brisana wasn't listening to her, but what she said was worse. Darcy knew there was truth to Brisana's words. There was something wrong with her, and it was affecting her sleep, her thinking, and her judgment.

"Brisana, I saw him in the car today. He was with some girl in a UCLA shirt. I'm telling you the truth."

"Darcy, that was his cousin, okay. Duane was picking her up after class," Brisana growled. "You got anything else you wanna say?"

Darcy felt a sinking feeling in her stomach, as if she'd swallowed a brick. "His *cousin*?" she repeated. It still did not make sense. She was sure that the girl had kissed him. "Are you sure? I thought I saw—"

"Darcy, just drop it!" Brisana yelled, cutting Darcy off. A second later, the phone went silent.

"Brisana?" Darcy asked, but she knew it was pointless. Brisana had hung up on her.

Without a second thought, Darcy called Tarah. The two had not spoken in days.

"I told you she wasn't gonna listen," Tarah said, "At least you know you did the right thing. You tried. That's more than most people would have done."

"I don't know. I just have a bad feeling."

"What else can you do? It don't take a genius to know that Duane is trouble. Cooper's about ready to quit his job, he's so fed up. I think that girl you saw was actually at the station today. Coop said Duane was showin' off all day, bossin' him around in front of some college girl. And from what Coop saw, those two ain't cousins, not unless they're *kissin'* cousins!"

"I knew it!" Darcy exclaimed. "That boy only wants Brisana for one thing, and she just doesn't see it." She could feel her pulse pounding in the side of her head. It was so loud she wondered if Tarah could hear it over the phone.

"Darce," Tarah said, the tone of her voice shifting suddenly like the gears of a car. "You mind if I ask you somethin'?"

"No, Tarah, what's up?"

"You're takin' all this business with Brisana real personal. I mean, I know you two were friends, but it seems like there's something else goin' on." Tarah spoke carefully, and Darcy could hear the sincerity in her voice. "Is everything all right with you?"

Darcy took a deep breath. "What do you mean?" she said, trying to pretend as if she did not understand her friend's question.

"C'mon, Darce. We're tight. We been hangin' all year, and I know when somethin's buggin' you. You ain't been yourself in weeks. You don't wanna come out anymore, and you always seem down. And I know about your grandma, but this stuff with Brisana is somethin' else."

Darcy knew Tarah meant well, but she could not bring herself to say the words. And she wasn't even sure what they were.

Brian attacked me. He almost raped me. Now I have these bad dreams, and I don't feel safe anymore. Guys make me nervous.

Everything she could think of sounded almost crazy. She felt as if she was making a big deal out of something that wasn't serious. That she should just keep the whole thing secret, just like Mom and Dad were doing about whatever was wrong with them.

You're acting like a baby, said a voice in her head.

It was what Brian said when his hands were slipping under her shirt, tugging at her clothes. She knew the voice was wrong, but it had power. It made her feel embarrassed and guilty and unable to speak about what happened. Not even to Tarah, the person she believed would never hurt her.

"Tarah . . . I've just been busy, that's all. I been working a lotta hours at Scoops, and I guess I been kinda tired," Darcy said. She felt guilty for not telling Tarah the full truth, but it was as if she had a hand on her throat, preventing her from saying what had really been bothering her for so long.

"Oh, but you're not too busy to go to

the mall with Brisana," Tarah replied, raising her voice slightly. "I understand completely."

"No, Tarah, it's not like that."

"Whatever, Darcy. I was tryin' to help you, that's all. If you can't talk to me, that's your problem."

Darcy could hear the hurt in Tarah's voice. She couldn't believe what was happening around her. The secret with Brian was a kind of cancer, spreading its way into her closest friendships. She had to tell someone soon. Maybe now.

"Look, Darcy, I gotta go," Tarah said suddenly. "You still have time to come with us tomorrow for the July 4th cookout, right? Or are you gonna be *busy*?"

There was no way Darcy could open up to Tarah now, not with the resentment she heard pushing through the phone at her.

"I'll be there, Tarah. Definitely," she said.

"All right. I'll see you then."

Chapter 7

Darcy looked around and realized she was in a dark room. She could see the brassy glint of a doorknob and reached for it, but it was locked. A candle burned on a small table in front of her, and then a wave of panic hit her as she recognized where she was: Brian Mason's apartment. She heard footsteps behind her. She knew it was him.

"Leave me alone!" she yelled.

"Shut up," Brian hissed, his face suddenly only inches from hers. "You're acting like such a baby," he said, moving his body closer in the dim light. She knew he was going to try to touch her again.

"Get away!"

His hands grabbed her leg, and she twisted away, opening her eyes and waking up in her bedroom. It was July 4th, Independence Day, and Darcy sat up in her bed covered in a layer of sweat not caused by the heat already building in the summer morning.

Suddenly she heard knocking at her bedroom door. The sound startled her so much she jumped to her feet and balled her hands tightly into fists as if she was preparing for a fight. "You okay, Darcy? I thought I heard you talking." It was Jamee.

"Yeah, I'm fine. Just a dream."

"Can I come in?"

Darcy opened the door to face her sister already dressed.

"Man, you look like you haven't slept at all, and it's almost noon. Are you sick or something?" Jamee asked. "You never sleep this late."

"No, I'm not sick," Darcy snapped, turning away so she didn't have to see her sister's concerned eyes. "I just had a long day yesterday, and I was tired."

"I thought maybe you had what Mom has."

"Huh?"

"She was sick early this morning. I heard her in the bathroom throwin' up. She even decided to stay home from work. But she's feeling better now. She's gonna go to the cemetery to visit Grandma, and since you're not working today, I thought you might want to go with us."

"I do," Darcy said without any hesitation. It was an idea that felt right, one that pushed away the memories of her nightmare like leaves before a strong gust of wind.

Darcy had not been to the cemetery since Grandma's funeral. Passing the gray rows of headstones reminded Darcy of the day weeks ago when she stood with her friends and family and watched Grandma's coffin being lowered into the ground. The memory still brought tears to her eyes.

Jamee walked next to her in silence, while Mom led the way, carrying a tissue which she dabbed into the corners of her eyes from time to time. Birds flew overhead, chirping cheerfully in the trees over the great field of graves.

"You know Grandma would be happy to hear the birds," Jamee said.

Mom sniffled slightly.

Darcy nodded.

Grandma's grave was more recent

than most of those around it. The grass over her plot did not match the surrounding ground cover, and a thin line was visible in the turf where the earth had been dug. Yet already new grass had begun to mend the scar in the soil. Flowers, old and new, were piled up against the flat slab of granite that bore Grandma's name: Annie Louella Duncan.

"I planted these last week with your father," Mom said pointing to several tiny purple flowering plants next to the plaque. "Grandma would like them."

Darcy imagined her parents at the grave together kneeling on the ground planting flowers. Though it was sad, the image comforted her, signaling that her parents weren't totally coming apart, even if they were having problems.

"There's nothing more important in this world than family," Grandma had said shortly after Dad returned. *"Even when they make mistakes—and they always will, Angelcake—you have to keep loving them back. That's what it's all about."*

Darcy wondered what Grandma would say if she knew what was happening in the house now. The awkward silence. The hushed conversations. The tension. And then there was Darcy's dark secret, which, with each passing day, seemed to seep like poison into every facet of her life.

I need help, Grandma, Darcy thought to herself, looking at the grave.

Jamee and Mom seemed to say their own silent prayers. Divided by their thoughts, the three of them stood together in front of Grandma in respectful silence.

At 5:00, Darcy took a shower and did her best to conceal the circles under her eyes. She had agreed to meet Tarah and Cooper at the park at 6:30. They would barbecue for a while, and once it got dark enough, they would grab a good spot to watch the fireworks. Darcy wished there was some way she could avoid going. She just wasn't in the mood to be out, even with Tarah, but she had no excuses. And she knew Tarah would be upset if she canceled. She had to go.

"It'll be good for you," Tarah had said. Darcy did not believe that at all. She hoped Tarah would decide not to bring her cousin Troy to the cookout. The last thing Darcy wanted was to have a stranger following her around all night,

even if he was Tarah's cousin.

Outside on the street, the air hung heavy and thick under the late afternoon sun. It was so hot, Darcy had originally decided to wear shorts and a tank top, but when she looked in the mirror, she decided to change. Her chest and round backside, which never bothered her before, made her feel self-conscious. Hakeem had often told her she had a great body, and his words used to make her feel attractive, but after Brian, she didn't want that kind of attention. It made her uncomfortable. She put on a loose-fitting T-shirt instead.

Nearing the park, Darcy could smell the heavy, meaty aroma of hamburgers and hot dogs cooking on grills. Children's laughter mingled with the sound of classic hip-hop as she turned the corner and looked for Tarah. Though it was still early, people of all ages had started gathering in the park, sitting in beach chairs or on towels. Others sat at card tables while family members grilled in the shade of the park's few tall trees. Some people were dancing playfully to the music, while others were just kicking back, watching people.

Police cars were positioned at each

corner of the park, and officers were keeping an eye on people as they passed by. At the far side of the park, a crowd of shirtless teenage boys played a sweaty game of basketball, while some girls looked on. Darcy had been to the park on Tarah's birthday early in the year, and she knew exactly where Tarah would be. She spotted her nearly a block away, standing behind a smoky grill with a spatula in her hand. A dark-skinned guy, about six feet tall, stood next to her.

"Troy! Grab me some rolls!" Tarah yelled to the guy at her side. Overhead, a cloud of smoke billowed into the sky.

Darcy cringed. Troy was there. The whole night, Tarah would be watching them, trying to get them to talk. Tarah, the unwanted matchmaker.

"Girl, give me one second," Troy protested. Facially, he had Tarah's wide nose and friendly eyes, but he was built skinny like Hakeem.

"One more second, and you're gonna have to eat burnt burgers," she replied.

Troy handed her the rolls and then noticed Darcy. "Hi," he said with a smile, checking her out. "You must be Darcy."

"That's me," Darcy said, returning

the smile to be polite. "And you must be Tarah's cousin, Troy."

"Girl, it's about time!" Tarah exclaimed, taking a step away from the smoky grill. "Troy, this is my girl Darcy that I was tellin' you about. Why don't you get her something to eat?" Tarah ordered.

Troy smiled and shook his head. "What'll it be? Hamburger? Hot dog? Chicken? Something to drink? We got all kindsa soda."

"I'll take a hamburger and a grape soda," Darcy said.

Before Troy could give Darcy the plate of food, Tarah took it and handed him a spatula. "Here, you cook for while," she instructed him. "I need to talk to my girl for a minute."

Tarah quickly stepped around the grill and pulled Darcy aside. "So whadya think? I know he's my cousin and all, but ain't he fine?"

Darcy nodded. It was going to be a long night, she thought to herself. "He seems really nice, Tarah."

"He thinks you're pretty too," Tarah said. "I can tell."

"Tarah," Darcy said, making sure not to sound upset or angry. "I'm not looking for a boyfriend."

"I know, Darce, and Coop told me that Hakeem's coming back this fall. But that's a long time away, and I just thought it would do you some good to hang out for once. Besides, Troy's not a player like most of the guys around here," Tarah said. "Hey, look who it is."

Darcy turned to see her sister and Desmond Hodden walking together holding hands.

"How you doin', girl?" Tarah said to Jamee, and then turned to Desmond, who looked like a miniature Cooper. "Where's your brother at? He's supposed to be here by now!"

"Far as I know, Coop's at the station. He said it was closing early, so he should be here any minute."

Desmond and Jamee went over to the grill to get some food. Darcy ate her hamburger and watched as Jamee clung to Desmond's arm. Several times, he put his hand on the small of her back. Watching them, Darcy almost felt like a parent.

"You know it's their one month anniversary tonight? I remember when me and Coop were like that," Tarah said.

"Yeah, well I just hope she knows

what she's doing," Darcy said.

"What do you mean by that?"

"She's my little sister, Tarah. I gotta look out for her. Last boyfriend she had hit her, and like you said, lotsa guys are players, only looking for one thing," Darcy admitted, thinking of Brian.

"Not Dez. He ain't gonna hurt her, Darcy. He's good people. Besides, Coop watches every move he makes. Believe me, that boy knows better than to misbehave with Coop around."

"Yeah, but where is Coop now?" Darcy said, watching Dez and Jamee cuddling on a bench.

Tarah looked insulted, but she didn't say anything.

Through the corner of her eye, Darcy saw a girl in a short skirt, sandals, sunglasses and a tight shirt that left her stomach exposed. It was Brisana. Next to her was Duane. They were holding hands too.

"Tarah, look who else is here," Darcy said, pointing at them.

"Now *there's* a player," Tarah said, watching them approach. "What does that girl think she's doin'? I ain't ever seen her tryin' so hard."

Just like the day at Scoops, guys in

the park turned to watch Brisana pass by. Darcy could not believe how much her friend had changed. The old Brisana would not allow a guy to tell her what clothes she should wear, especially not clothes that showed so much of her body. It wasn't Brisana's style. Yet what bothered Darcy more than the stares and the clothes was Brisana. Her face was blotchy, and she looked upset, as if she had been crying.

"She doesn't look happy," Darcy said, wondering what was wrong.

"No, she doesn't," Tarah agreed. "I bet I know who's responsible for that."

Overhead, the sky was beginning to darken, and the crowd continued to build. More police cars gathered on the edge of the park, visible under the street lights. Darcy recognized people from school around her, and then she noticed someone weaving through the crowd, moving rapidly in her direction. It was Cooper, but the smile always on his face was missing.

"Where you been? The fireworks are almost startin'."

"If I see Duane Nye here, I'm gonna bust him. I don't care how many cops are in this park," Cooper fumed. "Dude

91

blamed me for stealin' twenty dollars from the cash register. I know he took the money, but Mr. Nye wouldn't believe me. He made me clean up the whole shop to make up for it."

Suddenly Darcy heard a dull thud and noticed an orange fireball streaking like a comet into the sky.

"Here we go," Troy said, moving closer to Darcy. "I love watchin' fireworks."

BOOM!

The fireball exploded in a white flash with a blast like a hundred gunshots, making the ground shake. The crowd cheered as the rumble of the blast echoed through the park and into the surrounding neighborhood.

"Man, I don't even wanna be here," Cooper said. "I already got a headache."

"Just calm down and enjoy the show. There's nothing you can do now," Tarah said.

KA-BAM!

Another explosion cracked the night sky. Cooper grabbed a soda from Tarah's cooler and glared upward, taking a deep breath. Several smaller explosions thundered overhead, leaving fiery trails of shimmering green and red embers. In the flickering light, Cooper's tense face looked scary, almost demonic. Darcy shuddered. She had never seen him so upset. Everything about the night was making her edgy.

Behind her, under a nearby tree, Darcy spotted Jamee and Desmond. They were kissing each other, stopping only occasionally to look at the fireworks. Darcy shook her head in silent disapproval. She wanted to drag Jamee home and tell Dad what was happening, but she couldn't move. And yet, she couldn't stop staring.

Part of her wanted to protect Jamee. But she knew Desmond was the nicest boy her sister had ever dated. And kissing in the park was normal. It was only kissing. Still, the scene disturbed Darcy, making her feel an uncomfortable mixture of concern, fear, and worry. Yet there was also a tinge of jealousy. She didn't want what Jamee had. Not at all. Instead, she wished that she too could be normal like Jamee and feel comfortable with a boy. Yet now, after Brian, that seemed impossible. Even Troy, standing beside her, made her nervous.

"Looks like they are making some fireworks of their own," Troy said, following Darcy's gaze. "You can't blame them, though."

"I guess not," Darcy said, turning away from her sister and Desmond. She wished Troy would walk away and leave her alone.

Above them, the fireworks were peaking, exploding every few seconds. Troy turned his attention back to the sky, and Darcy glanced at Cooper. Tarah was rubbing his back, trying to calm him down. Darcy became aware that everyone else was part of a couple except her and Troy. He seemed to notice too.

"I'm really glad you came out today. I think I'd feel really lonely if you weren't here," Troy said, leaning close so she could hear him against all the noise.

Darcy squirmed. "I know what you mean," she said. If Troy had been anyone else, Darcy knew she would just walk away. But he was Tarah's cousin. She had to be nice to him.

A sudden rapid burst of smaller explosions signaled that the performance was coming to an end, but to Darcy the show couldn't end quickly enough. Clouds of foul smoke from the fireworks hovered over the park like a mysterious fog, hanging right above everyone's head.

Darcy felt Troy's hand gently wrap around hers.

Don't do this. Not now, she thought. *Please, not now.*

Troy looked at her with a smile, his friendly eyes curious and sincere. Darcy could feel that Tarah was watching her too, waiting to see what would happen. Tarah's presence made her even more nervous. Darcy's stomach began to tremble, and she could feel sweat beading on her forehead and back. Every instinct in her body told her to act.

Run away, it said. *Get away now.*

Another impulse, just as strong, urged her to yank away her hand and slap him. *Who said you could touch me?* it demanded. It was as if Troy had suddenly disappeared and Brian Mason had taken his place. Darcy scanned the park looking for an excuse to get away, to hide from the eyes that were on her, to remove herself from Troy's touch without making a scene.

Suddenly Cooper screamed out.

"There he is! I gotta do this *now*," he said, his voice recovering all the rage it had when her arrived straight from work.

"No, Coop! Let it go," Tarah urged,

trying unsuccessfully to stop him.

Darcy followed his glare and saw Duane Nye weaving through the crowd of people. Behind him, struggling to keep up, was Brisana. Darcy could see tears in her eyes.

Cooper was charging straight for Duane like a wild dog on the trail of its prey.

"Coop!" Tarah yelled. "Don't do it!"

But Darcy knew it was already too late.

Chapter 8

Darcy stepped away from Troy and watched Tarah dash into the park after Cooper.

"We better go after them," Darcy said, pulling her hand free. Troy nodded.

Without another word, they followed Tarah, who dodged through the crowd of people slowly exiting the park. Just ahead, Darcy could see Cooper shoving his way through the sea of people just as he did when he played football for Bluford High School.

"Slow down, homes," someone yelled as Cooper passed, but he ignored the comment. He was a missile streaking towards its target, but Tarah was right behind him.

"C'mon y'all. We gotta stop this," she yelled.

Duane and Brisana were just ahead of them, walking along the street which bordered the park. Duane moved briskly as if he was in a hurry to get somewhere. Brisana was behind him, struggling to keep up. Darcy could see her eyes glistening in the nearby street light.

Cooper darted in front of Duane's path, blocking him from going any further. Duane's eyes widened as if he was caught completely by surprise. Brisana's jaw dropped at the sight of Cooper, who glared menacingly at Duane.

Darcy, Tarah, and Troy arrived at the same instant, surrounding Cooper.

"C'mon, Coop. Let's just go home. He ain't worth it," Tarah said, grabbing Cooper's arm and trying to pull him away. He refused to budge.

"What are you all doing here?" Brisana asked, wiping her eyes and turning to Darcy. "What's going on?"

"Your boyfriend owes me twenty dollars and an apology. That's what's going on," Cooper said, scowling at Duane.

"Man, you just ain't smart, are you? No wonder you're gonna spend your whole life working at a garage in the 'hood," Duane said. "I don't owe you jack, and if you keep this up, I'll make sure you lose your job along with that twenty dollars you're looking for," he added. "Now c'mon, Brisana."

Cooper stepped closer, but Tarah jumped in front of him, turning to Duane with an anger Darcy had never seen before.

"Who you think you are, actin' like you all better than everybody? Without your Dad payin' for your school and your car, you're just another punk with a big mouth," Tarah said, putting her hand on her hip and shaking her head as she spoke. "And if you knew what was good for you, you'd leave Coop alone, 'cause he's the best worker your Dad ever had."

"Girl, I don't know what planet you're from, but you better shut that fat mouth of yours if you know what's good for *you*."

Cooper charged, but Darcy and Troy stood in his way, trying to hold him back. For a second, Cooper hesitated, and Darcy could see the veins bulging in his neck. It looked as if he would explode just like the fireworks a few minutes before. Troy had his hands on Cooper's chest, trying to keep him from moving forward.

"He's just a punk, Coop. He ain't worth gettin' in trouble over," Troy said.

"Yeah, I guess you're right," Cooper said, turning around as if he was walking away. Troy and Darcy stood back as he took several steps.

"Let's go, Coop," Tarah said, seeming relieved.

"Yeah, that's what I thought you'd do," Duane said, a satisfied grin on his face.

But then, with catlike speed, Cooper spun around and lunged at Duane.

Before anyone could react, Cooper slammed his shoulder into Duane's ribcage, tackling him to the ground. As Duane struggled to get to his feet, Cooper pounced on him, punching him twice, once in the face and then in the stomach.

"Get off me," Duane yelled, trying to protect his head from Cooper's punches.

The words struck Darcy like an arrow to her heart. She had used the same words when she screamed out against Brian just before her father came and saved her. Now Duane, a guy she despised, was trying to save himself from Cooper, one of Darcy's best friends. It was as if the world had been turned inside out, and yet Darcy could not just stand there. Not after what had happened to her.

"Both of you stop it," she yelled, rushing over and grabbing Cooper's shirt as he struggled with Duane.

"You owe me twenty dollars, and if you don't give it to me, I'm gonna take it," Cooper growled. It was like his rage had possessed him, taking away the Cooper Darcy knew and replacing him with this angry spirit.

"Let him go, Cooper," Darcy said, unable to stop herself.

Troy tried to grab her then, seizing her wrist and pulling her away. "Stay out of it, Darcy," he said. "It's dangerous."

Though Darcy knew Troy meant well, his grip hurt her, triggering a memory of when Brian forcibly grabbed her wrists and demanded she calm down, even as he refused to let her go. The pressure of Troy's fingers clenched on her wrist produced the same pain, the same sensation, the same panic. She couldn't control the scream that suddenly roared from her lungs, the horrific flashback that replayed in her mind, or the sudden kick she sent into Troy's groin. It all happened in a blinding flash.

"What's wrong with you?" Troy said as he sunk to his knees. "I was only trying to help."

Cooper and Tarah turned to face her. So did Brisana. Even Duane looked stunned.

"I'm sorry," Darcy said, ashamed to look at them all. "I couldn't help it."

Suddenly a shaft of light beamed through the trees from the edge of the park. It swept left and right, casting long eerie shadows of the trees and people in its path.

"Cops!" someone shouted.

"Oh no," Troy said.

"Man, get off me!" Duane hissed, wrestling beneath Cooper.

"Coop, unless you want us all to get in serious trouble, you need to let him go. *Now*," Tarah urged.

Cooper stood up as the swath of light from the police car moved closer. He paused, staring at Duane, who stood up rubbing his stomach.

"Let's go, y'all. They're gonna ask us a million questions if we stay here," Tarah said.

"Man, you might as well quit work tomorrow, 'cause I'm gonna make sure you're fired," Duane said, glaring at Cooper. "What I should do is have them cops come over here and arrest you. Everyone knows you just jumped me for no reason," Duane said.

"I didn't see nothin'," Troy said.

"Me neither," said Tarah, who looked at Darcy as if she expected her to go along with the lie they were prepared to tell.

"Yeah, well, Brisana is all the witness I need," Duane said. Everyone turned to look at her.

"Let's just go, Duane. I don't know what I saw," Brisana said, wiping her eyes again and walking away.

"Girl, you're trippin'! You know exactly what he did to me."

The spotlight focused on a tree just twenty feet away. The edges of the beam were close enough that Troy had to step back.

Tarah nodded at Brisana and turned away. "We outta here," she said. 'C'mon, y'all."

Troy, Cooper, and Tarah started walking away briskly, and Darcy watched as Duane trailed Brisana, who had headed off in the opposite direction.

"Girl, what is your problem?" Duane

demanded.

"You know exactly what my problem is, Duane," Brisana replied, their voices growing more faint as they walked away.

Darcy rushed to catch up to the group. She did not know what to say to Troy or to anyone else about what happened just moments earlier, though she knew she owed them some kind of explanation. Just thinking about how she screamed made Darcy feel stupid and embarrassed. When Troy grabbed her, something had snapped, revealing to everyone the fear that had, until then, been her secret. The scars of Brian's attack.

"Darce, you and me got to talk, but let's save it for tomorrow. I think we all better get home before we get in more trouble," Tarah advised, looking at Cooper, who was lost in his own thoughts. Watching him, Darcy thought he almost looked ashamed, as if he too had crossed a line he now regretted.

Together, they walked back to the grill, cleaned up the remaining food, and quietly left the park. Tarah led the way, making sure they walked slowly, careful not to attract the attention of the police who watched the remnants of the crowd dispersing from the fireworks show. Once the last of the police cars was behind them, everyone sighed, and Darcy turned to Troy, who had kept his distance from her during the entire walk.

"I'm sorry, Troy. It was an accident," Darcy said, trying her best to look at him.

"Whatever," he said bitterly.

In silence, they crossed several blocks and made their way through the neighborhood to Cooper's old pickup truck. Without a word, Troy jumped in the back, while Tarah and Darcy sat inside with Cooper.

"Well, at least we didn't get busted," Cooper said as he started the truck.

"Amen to that," Tarah added.

Minutes later, the noisy pickup lumbered to a stop outside Darcy's house. Darcy spotted her sister and Desmond sitting on the front step holding hands.

"Look at them two lovebirds. They musta walked home. I'm glad their evening was better than ours," Tarah said.

"Yeah, but I think it's time for that evening to end," Darcy said, looking at her watch. It was almost 10:30.

Jamee almost looked disappointed to see them, but Desmond stood up right away.

"Where were you?" Desmond asked, looking at his brother. "You just disappeared. I thought I was gonna have to walk home."

"Get in. We're goin' home now," Cooper said, offering no explanation. Desmond seemed to sense his brother was serious. He said something to Jamee and dashed over to the truck.

Darcy quickly got out and headed toward the house.

"I'll call you tomorrow, Darcy," Tarah said as the old truck revved up and pulled away.

"Weren't those fireworks great? Me and Dez had the best time," Jamee gushed. She spoke quickly, her voice so full of excitement she didn't wait for Darcy to reply. "And what about you and Troy? I saw him checkin' you out. He has a really cute smile. You guys looked good together too."

Darcy took a deep breath and fought the urge to lash out at her sister.

"I don't have time for this right now. I've gotta work tomorrow, and I'm tired," Darcy said walking into the house.

"*Wait a minute*," Jamee demanded, following her to the door of her room. "You gotta tell me what happened with you two tonight. Did you at least like him?" Jamee asked.

Suddenly the phone rang. Jamee rolled her eyes but then raced back to grab it. Darcy fled to her bedroom, eager to get away from her sister. She knew Jamee hadn't seen her kick Troy, and she hoped to keep it that way.

But a second later, she heard Jamee in the hallway. "It's for you, Darcy. It's Brisana. She sounds upset."

Darcy opened the door and took the phone. "Brisana?"

"I need to talk to you, Darcy," Brisana said, her voice shaky.

"Where are you? Did he hurt you?" Darcy asked, imagining her old friend fighting off an attack like the one she faced.

"No he didn't hurt me. I'm home. But I . . . I think . . ." Brisana's voice cracked, and Darcy heard her blow her nose. "Can you meet me tomorrow? I don't want to talk about this over the phone."

"Yeah, I'm working tomorrow, but I get my break at 4:00. I can probably get someone to cover for me for an hour or so. If you want to see me sooner, maybe I can—"

"I'll meet you at 4:00. I gotta go. I can't talk now." The phone clicked and then went dead. Brisana had abruptly hung up. Darcy could almost picture her, sitting somewhere alone crying.

What did he do to her? Darcy wondered. She could feel rage in her chest, anger at guys who hurt girls, guys who dealt with their problems by taking them out on those around them.

Yet even as she thought about Brisana, Darcy remembered Troy. He had been completely innocent, and she had lashed out at him for the same reason, hurting him because someone once hurt her. It was a cycle of pain that needed to stop.

Darcy knew she needed to talk to someone, at least to her parents. Maybe to Tarah. But the idea of admitting her fears, of exposing how weak and vulnerable Brian made her feel, was almost too much to bear. It made her feel like a helpless child. Her face burned with shame as she returned the cordless phone to the kitchen.

"Is Brisana okay? I never heard her that upset," Jamee said when Darcy hung up the phone.

"Yeah, she's fine, Jamee. Don't worry about her," Darcy lied. She knew better than to tell Jamee anything about her friends. If she did, the whole neighborhood would know about it in a few hours. Jamee loved gossip.

Jamee looked insulted, but Darcy rushed by her, hoping to get back into her room before her sister could say anything. As she got to the door, Darcy could hear Jamee's footsteps behind her.

"Darcy, you never answered my question. How did it go with Troy?"

"I told you I'm tired. I'm going to bed," Darcy replied.

"Darce, what is your problem?" Jamee asked, putting her hands on her hips and raising her voice. "You got nothin' but attitude anymore. The way you look at me it's like you can't stand me or something. You act like I'm doing something wrong even though I'm not."

Darcy knew there was truth in Jamee's words, but she wasn't ready to talk about it. Not now, not after hearing Brisana weep or seeing Cooper beat up someone in the shadows of the park. Not after what she had done to Troy.

"Good night, Jamee."

Darcy closed her bedroom door in Jamee's face, leaving her standing in the hallway alone. Jamee cursed angrily and stormed away. Darcy heard her bedroom door slam shut seconds later. She turned her lights out, guilt hanging in the air like a heavy cloud of smoke.

Chapter 9

"What'd you do last night, Darcy? Did you see fireworks?" Haley asked. She and Darcy arrived at Scoops at the same time, 11:55. Haley was already wearing her green apron.

"Yeah, you could say that," Darcy replied, putting on her Scoops visor. She was still tired from the night before. It had been another night of tossing and turning, but instead of nightmares, Darcy simply could not relax, her mind spinning with echoes of Brisana's pained voice and images of Cooper's rage.

"Me too. I met the coolest guy. His name's Greg. He's so cute," Haley beamed.

Darcy turned away so Haley wouldn't see her roll her eyes. "That's great," she

111

said, trying her best to sound sincere. Before Haley could say something else, Darcy grabbed a dishcloth and started cleaning and straightening up the counters. She was not in the mood for small talk, especially not about boys.

By 3:30, Darcy had managed to sweep the floors, scrub the counter twice, clean the windows, and replenish the supplies of napkins and plastic spoons. Tamika seemed delighted at her work, complimenting her several times.

"Darcy, you gotta stop workin' so hard," Haley joked at one point. "I'm getting' tired just watchin' you. Besides, you're making me look bad too."

"Listen, Haley, I need a favor. I gotta step out at 4:00 for a little while. Can you cover for me?"

"Yeah, I guess so. I mean, you did everything already." Haley said, pausing to study Darcy's face. "Is everything okay?"

"Yeah, everything's cool. Thanks, girl," Darcy said, annoyed that she had to tell another lie.

At 3:55, Darcy spotted Brisana coming up the street. She was dressed in jeans and a navy T-shirt, nothing like the clothes she had been wearing in recent days. Yet her face looked almost gray, and her eyes were swollen and puffy as if she had been crying. Darcy had never seen her look so weary.

"Haley, I'm takin' my break," Darcy said, heading out to meet her old friend.

"Hey, Darce," Brisana said, wiping her eyes. "I'm sorry I'm taking you away from work. I just didn't know where else to go."

"Please, it's no big deal, Brisana. You're more important to me than a job," she said, meaning every word. Darcy led Brisana around the corner and headed into the alley behind Scoops. It was much quieter than the main street, though from the pained look on Brisana's face, Darcy figured it almost didn't matter where they were. "Brisana what is it? What's wrong?"

"I need you to promise me you're not going to judge me or tell anyone what I tell you."

Darcy paused. How could she promise if she didn't know what it was? And yet, how could she say no to Brisana, who looked more desperate than ever? "Okay," she said. "I promise."

Brisana shook her head, but kept her eyes focused on the ground. "Darcy,

I really screwed up," she said. "You can't tell anyone. Not even my mom."

"I won't, Bris. What is it?" Darcy asked.

"I think . . ." Brisana stammered, looking all around as if she was afraid someone was listening to her. "I think I'm pregnant."

"*Pregnant?!*" Darcy repeated, louder than she meant to.

"Why don't you just scream it to everyone!" Brisana yelled. "Please, Darcy, don't freak out on me, 'cause if you do that, I don't know what I'm gonna do."

Brisana's voice struck Darcy. It was sad and defeated, almost like she was begging. Darcy could hardly believe her ears. Brisana Meeks was one of the best students at Bluford. She and Darcy had practically grown up together. They used to talk about the girls at school who got pregnant and dropped out. Brisana had even insulted them from time to time. She was the last person Darcy ever imagined getting pregnant.

"I'm sorry," Darcy said, putting her hand on Brisana's shoulder. "Are you sure?"

"My period is four days late . . . that's never happened before." Brisana said, beginning to sob. "I . . . I just don't know what to do."

"Did you tell your parents?"

"*No!* There is no way I can tell them, Darcy. They'll kill me. I'm supposed to go to college in two years, Darcy. I can't be pregnant! Could you imagine what everyone will say about me if people at Bluford find out? I'm gonna have to quit school. I just can't deal with it, Darcy. I can't," Brisana said, her voice cracking into sobs.

Darcy put her arms around her. "Just calm down, Brisana. We'll get through this. Maybe you're not pregnant," she said, stroking Brisana's head. "I'll run to the drug store and get you one of those home pregnancy tests, and—"

"No," Brisana interrupted. "I tried one of those things, and I spilled it on the bathroom floor. It was a mess, and I couldn't even read the results right. If I go through that again, I'm gonna lose it for real," she said, wiping her eyes.

Darcy gently rubbed Brisana's back, the news washing over her in waves.

"If I am pregnant, it's Duane's baby," Brisana continued, blowing her nose. "I know I shouldn't have listened to him,

Darcy. But he was just so nice to me. He made me feel so special. And when he told me he loved me, I made myself believe him. The whole thing was over for him in a few minutes, but look at me."

"Did you talk to him about it?"

"Yeah, I talked to him. Know what he said to me? 'Ain't mine. I don't even want to hear it.' I was like, 'But Duane, you're the only person I was ever with like that.' He said it wasn't his problem. It's like you tried to tell me. He's a player. He just wanted one thing, and he got it. I know he was cheating on me, too."

"Enough about him. That boy's a dog," Darcy replied, angry for Brisana. Though she didn't say it, Darcy knew how Brisana had been fooled. Brian had almost done the same thing to her, telling her just what she wanted to hear. That she wasn't alone. That she was attractive, desirable, special, and loved. After the attack, Darcy had learned that Brian already had a child, something he had kept hidden from her when they were together.

"What am I gonna do, Darcy? I am in so much trouble."

Darcy tried to think of an easy

answer to give Brisana, but nothing came to her. Of course, they would have to figure out if Brisana was pregnant, but how? They couldn't just go to the doctor, not without a parent. They were both under eighteen.

"We have to tell your parents."

"No, Darcy. Don't make me do that."

"We gotta tell someone so we can get to the doctor and figure out if you really are pregnant," Darcy insisted. Suddenly an idea struck her. *Tarah.* She worked at the community center. That's where the clinic was. Even though the two weren't friends, Darcy figured Tarah could at least point her in the right direction. "I think I should tell Tarah. She works at the Brown Street Community Center. She can tell us what to do."

"No," Brisana protested. "I don't want Tarah thinking I'm some kind of slut or something. That girl already hates me. She'll tell all of Bluford about how I got knocked up."

"Brisana, you got Tarah all wrong. She's not like that. There isn't anyone I would trust more with this." Brisana shook her head, looking totally defeated, as if the idea of telling Tarah was something she could not bear.

"I can't do this, Darcy. I can't have you tell her."

"Look, let me just talk to her and see what she says. I won't even tell her it's you. For now, just go home and relax. When I get home from work tonight, I'll call her. Then I'll call you. Don't do anything until you hear from me."

"Are you sure?" Brisana asked, her eyed glistening in the late afternoon sun. "I'm gonna trust you 'cause I don't know what else to do. I really don't."

"You can trust me, Bris. I got your back," Darcy said, giving her another hug. "You're not alone in this. You hear me?"

Brisana nodded, her tears falling quietly onto the hot sidewalk.

For the rest of the day at Scoops, Darcy could not shake her conversation with Brisana. It was like an earthquake had happened in her mind, forever shifting her entire world.

Brisana thinks she's pregnant.

The words, so simple yet so strong, stole away their childhood, erasing it completely. They were not kids anymore, even though they were still in school and Darcy was sure Brisana still had her favorite stuffed animal, a soft teddy bear, in her room. Darcy imagined Brisana clutching it in fear, looking for some comfort against the real world, a place where kids have kids. Where boys lie. Where stupid decisions can change an entire life. Or make a new one.

"I'm with you, Brisana," Darcy whispered, thinking of Duane and Brian. Just their names made her angry, two boys who seemed to not care who they hurt. Darcy wished they were just part of a nightmare, like ghosts or vampires. Things unreal. Yet they were real. Guys like them were everywhere.

But then there were good guys. Hakeem was one of them. So was Cooper. Maybe even Troy was, though Darcy wasn't ready to give him a chance.

Someday, when you're older, you'll find yourself a good man, Angelcake. Believe me, they're out there. But don't rush. When you are ready, years from now, you'll find one and settle down. You'll see," Grandma had once said.

It was a conversation they had in the park over a year ago, before Darcy had dated Hakeem, months before Dad returned. At the time, it made Darcy uncomfortable, like the discussions in health class about condoms and periods. It was just too much.

Now Darcy could never imagine herself settling down with anyone. Grandma's words seemed to describe some other world, a place Darcy didn't know, free of Duanes and Brians. Free of fathers who leave home for five years. Free of the nightly crying and tension she had witnessed in her house during the past few weeks.

"I can't wait to see Greg again," Haley said, jarring Darcy from her thoughts. She took off her apron and visor.

"I'm happy for you," Darcy mumbled, looking at the clock. It was 8:00, the end of their shift. Darcy felt a nervous tremor in her stomach. Tarah would be home already. Darcy rushed home to call her.

"There you are," Dad said as soon as Darcy walked in. "We've been waiting for you."

"Huh?" Darcy asked, watching her father walk into the small dining room next to the kitchen. The house was filled with the aroma of fresh baked chicken. It was one of Dad's "specialties," a dish he learned to cook in the years he was away from the family. Yet such meals were usually for special occasions, not a regular weeknight, especially not this late at night.

"What's going on?" Darcy asked, as she reached the dining room. To her surprise, Mom was seated at the table, which was crowded with plates and bowls. One large dish contained a steaming chicken, golden and fresh out of the oven. There was even a candle in the center of the table. Jamee was next to Mom, a puzzled look on her face.

"What do you mean 'What's going on'? We're having a family dinner," Dad explained, pulling her chair out formally. "Have a seat."

Darcy sat down and looked over at Jamee, who shrugged her shoulders slightly, signaling that she too was confused. Across from Jamee, Mom looked tense, tapping her fingers on the table nervously.

"Mom, you're never home this early. I thought you wouldn't be here until 9:00."

"I came home early. Your father and I wanted to talk to you both," Mom said, looking at Dad as if she wanted him to confirm what she was saying.

Darcy felt her pulse begin to race. There was no way she could talk to Mom about Brisana now. Not with Jamee and Dad listening. But worse, something serious was happening. It was the only reason Mom would come home from work early. Even Jamee seemed to sense something important was going on. Darcy could feel Jamee's leg bouncing nervously under the table. It was something she always did when she was tense. Jamee's eyes were on Dad, who glanced at everyone as if he was preparing to make a speech.

"Go ahead, Carl. Tell them," Mom said. "We've waited long enough."

Darcy braced for the worst. This had to be what Mom had been upset about for so long, the strange problem that kept her parents up each night talking. The mysterious secret that, until now, had left her mother crying and her father unable to talk.

Dad took a deep breath and cleared his throat. Darcy tried to guess what was happening. Was it that he was fired and they were going to have to sell their house and move back to the apartment? Was it that Dad and Mom's decision to get back together wasn't working out?

Were they going to separate again? Darcy glanced back at Jamee, whose eyes were focused unblinking on Dad's face.

"Your mother and I have something important to tell you, something that's gonna change a lotta things around here," Dad said.

"It's not anything bad, is it?" Jamee asked. "Darcy said—"

"No, it's not bad, but it's not going to be easy for any of us, and we're gonna need both of your help."

"Is everything okay? Is someone sick?" Darcy asked, totally confused.

"No, no one's sick, Darcy," Mom cut in. "We're expecting a baby. I'm pregnant."

Darcy's jaw nearly detached from her skull and tumbled to the floor.

"*What?*"

"*For real?*" Jamee screamed, standing up from the table as if she couldn't contain what she had just heard. "Are you serious?"

"She's serious, all right. Your Mama's already two months along. She's due in February," Dad said, his face breaking into a smile. "You two are going to be big sisters."

Darcy sat back, unable to comprehend what her parents just said, her hands pressed to her cheeks in shock.

"Are you all right, Darcy?" Mom asked.

Darcy's mind spun at the news, the secret that had been hidden from her, one that had made her worry for weeks. She almost felt as if her parents had lied to her. As happy as she was with the news, she was also overcome with relief and hurt.

And her own secret, suddenly thawed by emotion, burned painfully in her chest ready for release. No more lies, she thought.

"No, Mom," Darcy admitted. "I'm not all right."

Chapter 10

Everyone at the table turned to Darcy as if she had screamed out a curse in the middle of dinner.

"Darcy, what are you saying?" Jamee asked.

"I'm saying I'm *not* all right," Darcy repeated, her hands beginning to tremble. "What about that didn't you understand?"

"Darcy, you got problems," Jamee protested. "This is the best news ever. Why can't you just be happy for once?"

Darcy shook off the tears that threatened to well in her eyes. "You just don't get it, Jamee. You never do."

"Darcy what's wrong?" Dad asked. "I thought you'd be thrilled at the news."

"I am, Dad, but you guys shouldn't have kept this from us, not for this long," Darcy said, wiping her eyes. "For weeks you've been walking around like something was wrong, and whenever I asked you about it, you said it was nothing. You guys were lying. And I could see it in your eyes," Darcy admitted. "I was worried. Like maybe you were about to split up again or something."

Jamee turned away, unable to hold Darcy's gaze.

"I'm sorry, baby," Mom said, reaching across and grabbing Darcy's hand. "But I'm not young anymore, and lots of things can go wrong. We were waiting to see what the doctors said, and, to be honest, it was a big decision for your father and me."

"It's a big decision for *all* of us," Darcy countered. "Before Grandma died, we used to talk about everything. Even though things were tough, we were a family. Now you never talk to us. It's like we're strangers in this house. You don't even ask me what I'm doing anymore. Instead, you're always too tired or stressed, or I don't know what," Darcy said, frustrated at her own words. She didn't want to accuse her parents or push them away. She just wanted them closer, yet she couldn't bring herself to ask. A tear rolled down along her cheek.

Darcy's mother nodded, getting up from the table and walking over to Darcy. "Oh, baby, I am so sorry," she said, putting her arm on Darcy's shoulder. "We didn't know what we were putting you through. I know things have been rough around here since Mama passed away, but believe me, there is nothing more important to your father and me than you two. And that's never gonna change. You hear me?"

Darcy looked up into her mother's eyes. She was surprised to see tears in them. Dad was next to her and Jamee next to him. They were all staring at her with concern and love. Darcy's heart ached for them, for her deceased grandmother, for the family they once were and could still be. She wiped her eyes.

"Jamee's right about me," Darcy said, turning away from their intense gaze. "I *do* have problems."

"I didn't mean it, Darcy," Jamee said. "I'm sorry."

"But you were right."

"What are you saying, Darcy? There's nothing wrong with you."

"No, Dad, there *is*."

"Baby, tell us what you mean," Mom

said.

Darcy shook her head, no longer able to hide her own dark secret, her fears. "Something happened to me that day . . ." Darcy paused, angry at how vulnerable and crazy she sounded. "That day I was attacked by Brian."

Dad's forehead creased with concern, and he kneeled down next to her. Jamee looked stunned, as if someone had slapped her in the face.

"I'm just not the same, Mom. I can't sleep. I get nervous when I'm around guys, and I'm scared all the time. So scared," she said, a great tide shifting in her chest. "I don't know what to do."

"Why didn't you tell us about this?"

"I guess I wanted to keep it secret. You guys seem so stressed all the time. I just didn't want to make things worse for you, but I can't hide it anymore," Darcy admitted, beginning to sob. "I need help, Mom," she said, tears flowing freely from her eyes. "I need help."

Darcy felt Mom's arms wrap around her tightly, and she closed her eyes. It was as if she was a child again, safe in Grandma's arms.

"We're gonna get you the help you need, baby," her mother said. "I know some good counselors at the clinic and at the hospital. Everything's gonna be all right. I promise you."

For a time, Darcy sobbed as the stress and worry in her mind gradually gave way to relief, and the night's news slowly began to sink in.

"I can't believe you're having a baby," Darcy said, looking up at her parents. "We really are a family aren't we?"

"Yes we are, and we're about to get bigger," Dad said.

"I wish Grandma was here," Jamee said. "This would make her so happy."

"I know, Jamee, but don't worry. I told Grandma all about this before she died. She knew before your father did," Mom said with a smile. "You know what she said? 'I always imagined you with three kids, Mattie. Now I know why.'"

Weary after the family dinner, Darcy took the cordless phone, went into her room and dialed Tarah's number.

"Hello?"

"Tarah, it's me. I need to talk to you," Darcy said.

"Girl, it's about time. I been meanin' to call you, but I just got off the phone with Coop. Turns out old Larry Nye didn't fire him. So many workers complained about Duane that his Dad decided to kick him out of the garage. I guess it's true. What goes around comes around," Tarah said.

"That's cool," Darcy said nervously, trying to find the right way to say what was really on her mind.

"Darce, what's going on?" Tarah asked. "I ain't never seen you as upset as you were last night. You got me worrying over here."

"Tarah, I have a lot of explaining to do," Darcy said, taking a deep breath. "I'm so sorry for what happened with Troy, and for acting so weird lately. I never told you this, but something happened to me after Hakeem left."

Without holding anything back, Darcy recounted the whole story about Brian Mason, from the moment they met to the time he attacked her. Before Tarah could even respond, Darcy explained how the attack changed her, leaving her edgy, unable to rest. She then told her about the panic attack and the episode in the park with Troy. "I just couldn't control it, the way he grabbed me."

"Aw, Darce, why didn't you say something to me, girl? I knew somethin' was eatin' at you, that you were unhappy. I could see it on your face as plain as day. Honestly, I was gettin' scared," Tarah said.

"I didn't want you to know. I guess I was afraid of what you'd think."

"Girl, I understand that, but I'm your friend. You shouldn't keep secrets from the people that care about you. We're just here to help. That's why God made us friends and put us in this crazy world together," Tarah said, her words strong and pure, as if they came straight from her heart.

"Besides, I know some real good people where I work that help girls all the time who are dealin' with stuff like this. Whenever you're ready, let me know. Counselors are there all the time every day. I'll even go with you if you want."

"Are you serious?"

"Of course I am! What kinda friend would I be if I didn't?"

"Tarah, you're the best," Darcy said, suddenly feeling relieved, as if Tarah had just taken a great weight off her shoulders.

"I know. That's what Coop says all the time," she said with a laugh.

Darcy sighed, grateful Tarah was in

her life. She had become more than just a friend. She was like another sister. But then Darcy thought of Brisana and how, not far away, she was home, waiting for a phone call, looking for help from a friend. Hoping for an answer from Darcy.

"There's something else I gotta ask you."

"Shoot, girl. I'm listening."

"A friend of mine thinks she might be pregnant. She doesn't know where to go, and she made me promise not to tell anyone."

Tarah suddenly got quiet, and Darcy knew what she was thinking. Of course, Tarah would figure it out. Who else could it be? But at least Darcy had followed Brisana's wishes, keeping her name hidden. Tarah would understand that.

"Is she okay, Darce?" Tarah asked, her voice filled with concern.

"She needs to find out. She's upset."

"Tell her to go to the clinic and see Dr. Styles. If you go in early, you should be able to see her. She's the one all the teenage girls go to. She'll be in tomorrow," Tarah said. "Darcy, if the test is positive, they're gonna have to contact her parents."

After a brief talk on the phone, Darcy convinced Brisana to meet her in front of the Brown Street Community Center at 8:30 a.m.

"I'll be there with you every step of the way. I promise," Darcy said, until Brisana reluctantly agreed to go.

Out on the street, the air was cool and clear, but the morning sun already glowed overhead with yellow fire. In a few hours, it would be a hot summer day. Darcy could feel it.

For a second, as she made her way to the clinic, Darcy wondered if Brisana would even show up, but then she spotted her walking down the street, her eyes dark and stormy.

"I'm scared. What if I'm pregnant, Darcy? What am I gonna do?"

"Let's just wait and see what happens," Darcy said as they walked into the glass and stucco building. The main hallway led to a corridor lined with door labels that made Darcy cringe.

Family Planning Office. Rape and Abuse Crisis Center. Counseling and Psychological Services Office. The signs made her tremble, reminding her of her own demons and the counseling she would need for herself. But that would happen another day. At the end of the hall, Darcy spotted the sign she wanted: Medical Clinic.

"This way," she said, guiding Brisana gently, her hand on her back.

They stepped into a waiting room with a gray tile floor and muted pink walls. Against the far side of the room was a row of plastic chairs and a table full of magazines. A small TV was bolted overhead in the far corner of the room. It was tuned to a morning talk show that Darcy didn't recognize. Straight ahead was a receptionist in a white shirt, holding a clipboard.

"Can I help you?"

"Yeah, we're here to see Dr. Styles," Darcy said. She could feel Brisana shaking.

"Are you sisters? Is one of you over eighteen?" the woman asked.

"No, we're friends. I'm sixteen, and I'm afraid I'm pregnant," Brisana said, her voice shaky and rough. "Can I please see the doctor?"

The receptionist nodded understandingly. "Normally, we don't see people who are under eighteen without a parent, but I'll see what the doctor says. For now, fill these out," she said and handed Brisana some forms.

Darcy led Brisana to a seat and helped her complete the paperwork and return the sheets to the receptionist. "I'm so glad you're here with me, Darce. I don't know what I'd do without you."

"It's okay, Brisana, I'll probably be coming back here soon myself," Darcy admitted.

"What do you mean?"

Darcy told Brisana about Brian and the attack, and how she planned to get help at the center. It was the third time she had repeated the story, but already it had less of a grip on her, as if each time she told it, she healed a little bit. "You were the only one who warned me about Brian. You tried to help, and I never listened. I'm just returning the favor," Darcy said.

"Oh, Darcy," Brisana said, stunned at the news. "I'm so sorry that happened to you. "

"It's okay," Darcy replied, swallowing her own emotions.

"Brisana Meeks," a firm voice said, breaking their conversation. A young, dark-skinned woman with braids pulled tight behind her head stood over them with a warm smile. "I'm Dr. Styles. Can you come with me?"

"Sure. Can I bring my friend?"

"Absolutely," she said, leading them back into a small examination room. The room was lined with medical posters. One of them was titled *Female Reproductive System*, and looked like something out of Darcy's health class textbooks from eighth grade. "So tell me why you're here," Dr. Styles said, directing Brisana to sit on the room's small examination table.

"I think I might be pregnant. I was with this boy. We weren't careful, and now my period's five days late," Brisana said, as if she was ashamed.

Dr. Styles nodded thoughtfully and quickly examined Brisana, listening to her heartbeat, taking her pulse, and checking her eyes, ears, and throat. "Let me guess," she added. "Your parents don't know, and the boy doesn't want anything to do with it."

Brisana nodded, wiping her eyes.

"Well, you're not alone, and you came to the right place, which is one good thing. Another good thing is that you seem completely healthy. Now, the pregnancy test is painless and easy. You'll know in a few minutes. The hard part will be if you are pregnant, but let's do the test first. I need you to go to the bathroom, and urinate in this," the doctor said, holding out a small plastic cup. Brisana looked squeamish but took the cup and headed to the bathroom. A moment later, she came out with the cup, and the doctor took it and disappeared.

"I'm so scared, Darcy."

Darcy put her hands on Brisana's back reassuringly, though she was worried too. Dr. Styles returned after a few minutes. The room suddenly felt charged like the sky a second before a lightning strike.

"Brisana, have you been nervous the past week or so?"

"Yeah, why?"

"Because your test came back negative. You're not pregnant. Sometimes, if you're really nervous or upset, you can make your period irregular. If you don't get it in a week, I want you to give me a call," the doctor said.

"You mean . . . *I'm not pregnant?*" Brisana asked, as if she didn't believe the words. Darcy sighed with relief.

"Nope. But if you keep doing what you did, you will be. I see too many girls your age in here each day not to use my time to give you a little advice. First of all, you don't have to have sex. No one ever got hurt from waiting a while.

"At the very least, if you are thinking about sex, take the time to make sure you know the person you are with, to make sure he deserves you and isn't using you. And if you do decide to have sex, *never* do it without protection. Besides pregnancy, there are diseases, and young people just like you get sick every day for no reason. We don't need any more suffering in this world. You gotta be careful.

"And one last thing: if some boy starts telling you he loves you so he can get busy, you need to get away from him. 'Cause if he truly loved you, he wouldn't be pressuring you like that. Got it?"

Brisana nodded.

"Good. Now we got counselors across the hall you can see if you want to talk to someone, and you can always find me here if you have questions. But to tell you the truth, it would make me happiest if I saw you in five or ten years with a good man at your side," she said with a smile. "Then pregnancy will be what it was meant to be. Good news. You hear me?"

"Thanks, Doctor," Brisana said, as if she had suddenly been freed from prison.

As they left the office, they passed through the waiting room. Several young women waited anxiously in the plastic chairs. One teenaged girl was seated exactly where Brisana had been when she first came in. An older woman, probably her mother, sat next to her. Neither of them said anything, but neither of them had to. Darcy knew exactly what they were there for. So did Brisana.

"Not every test comes out like mine, does it?" Brisana said knowingly as they left the office.

"No, it doesn't," Darcy replied, noticing a second hallway leading to the side of building. A sign overhead read, "Little Learning Spot Community Daycare Center—Use Entrance at Rear of Building."

"That's where Tarah works. I should stop and see her," Darcy said. "You can wait here if you want."

Brisana paused for a second. "No. I should thank her. I know she figured it out. She's not stupid."

Darcy smiled. Another secret was being washed away. "Good. Let's go."

Together Darcy and Brisana walked around the outside of the building. As they turned toward the back entrance, Darcy heard the laughter and cheerful screams of children. Up ahead, a metal fence surrounded a small playground full of little kids. Several adults were watching them play. Darcy spotted Tarah immediately. She was leaning over, playing with a little boy next to a sandbox. He looked to be about three years old, Darcy thought.

The boy was holding a plastic shovel, using it to build a little hill. Tarah tended to him carefully, asking him questions, and making sure he wasn't getting too dirty. Darcy didn't want to disturb her, but then Tarah saw them through the corner of her eye.

"Give me one second, J.J. I'll be right back," Tarah said, walking over to greet them. She looked back and forth as if she was trying to figure out what to say.

"Everything's okay, Tarah," Darcy said, careful not to reveal too much, just in case Brisana wasn't ready.

"The test was negative," Brisana said, looking straight at Tarah, a person who had once been her enemy. "It's the first test that I ever failed, but I'm not complaining."

"Amen to that," Tarah said. "I love kids, but when 5:00 comes, I'm ready to leave. When you're a mom, the job is 24-7. No time off. Not unless you got lotsa help. I don't know if I'm ever gonna be ready for that."

"Me neither," Brisana agreed.

J.J. tossed a shovel of dirt onto his pants and grinned as if it was exactly what he wanted to do. Tarah shook her head.

"Well, while you two are waiting for your own kids, you can come to my house," Darcy said.

Brisana and Tarah looked at her and then looked at each other in confusion.

"Darcy, what are you talking about?" Brisana asked.

"My mom's pregnant, and in February, there's gonna be another member of the Wills family. You two can help babysit."

Tarah and Brisana's jaws dropped and both girls hugged Darcy.

"Congratulations!" they cheered together. Darcy closed her eyes, squinting back tears and enjoying the embrace.

The summer's secrets had finally lost their grip. The distance that once separated her from her friends and family had vanished like fog beneath the bright sun. While the scars from Brian's attack lingered, Darcy knew she would spend the summer dislodging them. She would heal.

Looking at the warm smiles on her friends' faces, Darcy heard Grandma's words echo like music in her heart.

"Everything's gonna be okay, Angel-cake. You'll see. You're gonna be just fine."

And for the first time since the summer began, Darcy knew the words were true.

Have you read the other books in the Bluford Series?

(continued on the following pages)

A Matter of Trust

Anne Schraff

DARCY
+
HAKEEM

B L U F O R D   S E R I E S   TP

Secrets in the Shadows

Anne Schraff

BLUFORD SERIES **TP**

BLUFORD SERIES TP

Until We Meet Again

Anne Schraff

Paul Langan & D.M. Blackwell

Blood Is Thicker

BLUFORD SERIES TP

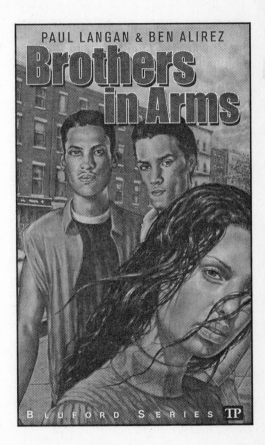

PAUL LANGAN & BEN ALIREZ

Brothers
in Arms

B L U F O R D   S E R I E S   TP

If you like the Bluford Series, you may be interested in other books in the Townsend Library:

Narrative of the Life of

FREDERICK DOUGLASS

An American Slave

Written by Himself

TP THE TOWNSEND LIBRARY

(continued on the following pages)

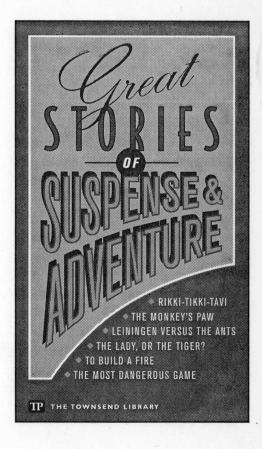

Great
STORIES
OF
SUSPENSE &
ADVENTURE

◆ RIKKI-TIKKI-TAVI
◆ THE MONKEY'S PAW
◆ LEININGEN VERSUS THE ANTS
◆ THE LADY, OR THE TIGER?
◆ TO BUILD A FIRE
◆ THE MOST DANGEROUS GAME

TP THE TOWNSEND LIBRARY

JACK LONDON

White Fang

TP THE TOWNSEND LIBRARY

READING
CHANGED MY LIFE!

THREE
TRUE
STORIES

Beth Johnson

THE TOWNSEND LIBRARY

**For more information, visit us at
www.townsendpress.com**